I0735632

GOOD GIRL

LEXIE MIERS

1

The opulent ballroom drew Emily Sander's eye like a bee to a daisy, her mouth agape as she continued to stare at her surroundings. She was technically in Melbourne, Australia, but if she used her imagination, she could easily see herself standing in an ancient castle.

"I can't believe how beautiful it all is."

The white silk draped over tall windows that reached up to the twenty-foot ceilings reminded her of gauze curtains and a four-poster Arabian Nights bed. The romantic lighting made the parquet floor positively gleam and she let a long sigh escape as her eyes feasted on the colors and textures of the fundraiser. It made her heart soar and her usually busy mind clear.

"I know. You never quite get used to the money they spend on these events."

Emily snapped out of her daze and turned to her companion for the evening, her supervisor and friend of several years. Why did she have to be so negative all the time? "What do you mean?"

Kristy rolled her heavily made up eyes and reached for a champagne flute which had swallowed a strawberry, as it travelled by on a tray carried by an attractive young waiter. He stopped and raised an eyebrow to Emily, but she smiled and shook her head. She had to work in the morning and her head was already spinning.

"I mean, look at it all." Kristy made a sweeping gesture with her hand that encompassed the free-flowing alcohol, five-piece band and hundreds of guests dressed in designer gowns and suits. "If they put all that money directly into the charity instead of wasting half of it on food and alcohol..."

Emily cringed as her eyes took another, more jaded glance around the gorgeous room. Kristy did have a point, but she was having such a great time she didn't really want her friend to ruin it.

"Not to mention the hair, makeup and shoes." Emily said under her breath.

"Exactly." Kristy pointed at her, taking another sip of her champagne.

Emily glanced around the room once again, the smiles and laughter all around her tugging a smile to her own lips. "But if they just donated the money, we couldn't hold the silent auction, which raises even more money, or meet any of the people who make all of this possible."

Kristy rolled her eyes at Emily once again, but a reluctant smile graced her lips.

"You are far too naïve for this world, Em. You aren't going to cope."

Emily shrugged and smoothed down her fitted bodice, which was a little tight for her normal level of comfort.

You're wrong, my friend.

Life had taught her early on that people could be cruel and unfair, but she hoped to be changing that, one person at a time. Her parents' failed marriage had left a scar or two that her past boyfriends had probably felt on occasion, but she tried not to let it overly affect her future.

She gave Kristy a cheeky wink as she allowed the butterflies to flutter in her stomach once more. This was her first big fundraiser for the women's shelter she'd been working with for over a year now. Her way of giving back to her community. She considered it her karma, although at times she was so tired she could barely speak. Which was why tonight gave her such a buzz. She worked more than ninety hours a week. This rare social outing thrilled her to her fingertips.

"Kristy, you know I'm a people person. Why wouldn't I be able to handle a few rich people?" She fluttered her eyelashes for effect at Kristy, who now stood in front of her coughing over the champagne which had obviously gone down the wrong way.

Kristy dabbed carefully at her nose and mouth with a white napkin. "Ah… because you seem to be more comfortable at Eleanor's House with the homeless, than anywhere else."

Emily straightened her shoulders and tossed her tresses. The pins holding part of her long hair up on top of her head were a little painful, but the beautiful glide of her blow-dried hair over her bare shoulders reminded her just how dressed up she really was.

"So true. But I'm going to do it anyway."

Another solid laugh came out of her friend's mouth.

Emily turned around and looked back at the room, twinkling crystal and mood lighting making the horn players on the stage seem otherworldly. A shiver coursed down her spine and a grin settled on her mouth. She didn't care what Kristy said about how excessive this night was, it was still pretty awesome.

A man she didn't recognize moved near and snared Kristy's attention while a pressure in Emily's body reminded her she'd drunk far too much water and champagne in the past hour.

She made her excuses and moved through the ballroom and into the bathroom, swaying her hips to the music and singing a little as she went. The ladies' room, which had a mirrored powder room with a central seat and then another door that led into the actual toilet, was as grand as the ballroom. She stared up at the carved ceiling and a sigh left her that would have made any fifties movie star proud.

No one had powder rooms anymore. The extravagance made her feel like she'd stepped back in time and as she wandered into the other room, she giggled to herself, happy and relaxed for once.

Her hands smoothed her dress down once more and she pushed open the heavy wooden door to re-enter the party. As she walked out of the ladies' toilet, someone exited the men's room at the same time. They crossed paths and suddenly she was lurching backwards as the black silk of her long dress was pulled down her body.

"Ow. My dress!" Emily bent forward and clasped her boned bodice to her chest. The shoestring strap on her right shoulder had snapped with the impact and had now fallen over her breast.

Oh, crap!

"Are you all right?"

Emily groaned as anger flowed through her. She lifted her eyes to the suited man standing over her, his hand on her arm burning into bare skin while his bright blue eyes narrowed with concern.

Her pulse quickened in her throat as her anger quickly drained away.

Oh, wow.

"Ah… yeah… you stepped on my dress."

"I'm very sorry. I didn't see you."

She stood up straighter, holding tightly to her bodice with one hand. Her generous breasts swelled against the silk and her belly tightened. Her eyes met his directly and her breath caught in her chest.

The man before her was simply beautiful, like James Dean had been back in his day. An angel in a bad boy suit. The epitome of every woman's desire and fear. She swallowed hard as her long-held prejudices about men warred with the lustful woman inside her. So few women ever tamed a man like this and she was the last woman who'd want to try.

His brow furrowed as he stared at her chest and she stepped back from his scrutiny. She brought her other hand up to her dress and lifted the broken strap.

"Is the strap completely snapped?" He stepped closer once again and inspected the damage, taking the fabric from her fingers and moving to her side to drape it back over her shoulder.

Emily couldn't breathe. Her heart pounded in her ears and her chest constricted. His touch on her sensitive skin made tingles skate over her, followed by a wave of heat. It had been way too long since she'd felt this.

"Ah, um, yeah, I think so. And it doesn't stay up so well without them." She pressed her hand to her stomach, swallowing hard as the man ran his fingers over her skin.

"I might be able to help you."

She glanced down as he pulled out a silver safety pin from his pocket.

A grin rose as she let some of the tension relax out of her body. Maybe this guy was more human than she'd originally thought? "No way. Are you a Boy Scout or something?"

He chuckled, his eyes sliding away as though the compliment made him bashful.

Oh, how gorgeous!

"This should fix it."

She held her breath and forced herself to stand still as his fingers pulled the dress away from her skin near her shoulder blades and pinned the strap back into place. The man's dexterity and speed with the pin quite impressive.

Emily sucked in her stomach and stared at the ornate ceiling, the heat from his fingers nearly burning her skin. This was a too much like a movie.

When he was finished, he stepped back and bowed to her as a chivalrous gentleman of old would. "My lady, my work here is done."

Emily clapped her hands and grinned at him, her excitement bubbling up for everyone to see. This guy was so different from the norm. Who was he?

"Oh, thank you so much. I'm Emily by the way."

She stuck out her hand and waited. The man who had just helped her out of a fashion *faux pas* stared at her for a minute with that look of surprise she often saw on people's faces when they met her. It was as though they'd never seen a happy person before. Well, she was no fake, so she continued to smile at him until he finally held out his own tanned, strong hand and shook hers firmly.

"I'm Nate."

"Nice to meet you, Nate."

Someone's approach cut into their exchange and Emily regretfully let go of his hand. She let her arm fall back to the side of her body as a woman rushed up to them, her red stilettos clicking on the polished floor.

"Nathan, we need you for some schmoozing." She reached for his tie and tugged it so that it was skewed further to the right and then back to the center.

It looked fine to begin with.

Nate grimaced but didn't pull away from the woman in red's polished fingers, his blue eyes straying to Emily's once again.

Emily jumped to get his attention for one more second before the blonde in red hauled him away. "Thank you so much again for your help."

He shrugged and opened his mouth as though he was going to respond, but the blonde slid her hand into the crook of his elbow and tugged. "Come on, you've been away from the room too long."

They walked away and Emily finally let her shoulders drop. Thanks to her father, she had a natural propensity to distrust men, so the fact that she'd met one that she'd liked, who didn't set off her internal alarm made her want to go after him. It would be such a waste not to talk to him a little bit more.

You're here to meet the people who give those women a home. This is business!

"Okay, okay."

She took a deep breath and calmed herself, her fingers tingling as she shook out her hands in front of her. She hadn't felt that instant attraction to someone in–well—ever.

Blowing out another long breath, she lifted her chin and walked back into the room. Her eyes scanned the crowd not for Kristy, but for the man in the black suit, patterned black tie and oh, so delicious blue eyes.

"Where'd you go?" Kristy sidled up beside her and handed her another glass of champagne.

She took it and lifted her other hand, running her nails softly over her lips, savoring the sensation of attraction that poured through her. It had been so long since she'd slept with anyone and although a one-night stand was the last thing she craved, it was so nice to feel *that* again. The awareness of her femininity, her nipples tingling beneath her dress. She craved that man's hands on her skin once again and part of her brain was working out how she could do both her job and manage to talk to Nate once more.

"Who are you looking at?"

Her eyes found him and her tummy jumped. "The guy in the suit over there."

Kristy chuckled. "Ah, which one of the hundred black suits before us?"

She lifted her chin a notch, her eyes pinned on "Nate." He moved around the room with the blonde, speaking to almost everyone he passed. He must be someone of some importance.

Hmm…

She frowned as he air-kissed the women he spoke to and shook hands with all the men. The fake smile he plastered onto his face did not reach his eyes. Even she could see it—all the way across the room. "Him. The one who's walking around the room with the woman in the red dress."

A gasp beside her and a snorting laugh made her pull her eyes away from him. A cold sickness was worming itself into her belly that she didn't appreciate at all. "What are you laughing at?"

Kristy's eyes practically bulged out of her head. "Don't you realize who that is?"

"No."

"That's Nathan Johnson. The billionaire. The man who built Eleanor's House and the reason you're here tonight."

What? No way.

"But… Huh?"

Heat flushed over Emily's body like a tidal wave. Starting at her neck, it spread up over her face and scalp. A storm of prickling, hot embarrassment. Nathan Johnson had always been a fantasy to her. A dream inside her head of what a man could be. And thus she'd acted like an excited child in front of him.

Obviously, he was successful and had an incredible philanthropic side. He was also so handsome he made her body throb, but that was secondary to his character. She'd found her perfect hero, but he was also her boss, sort of. Or was he? She couldn't work it out, but that might cause a huge issue if the attraction was reciprocated.

An older man stepped up and began engaging Kristy in conversation and Emily turned towards them, trying to concentrate on the man in front of her when all of her senses were trained on Nathan Johnson, who was heading her way. She shivered and clasped her hands in front of her, her heart beating a steady and increasingly hard tattoo against her ribs.

"And you work at Eleanor's House also?" The gentleman in front of her asked.

The hairs on the back of her neck prickled and she gulped before answering. He was close. "Yes, I'm a solicitor. I offer my services pro bono to the women at the shelter."

"Oh, and why is that?" A familiar, deep male voice asked from behind her.

Emily swallowed her moan as she shifted and they all stepped back to allow Nate and his handler to enter the circle.

She turned towards him, her belly tightening much lower than her navel. He'd asked her a question hadn't he? Oh yeah, that's right. "Because I believe that all women have the right to good legal counsel, irrespective of their financial situation."

She smiled at him with warmth, but he didn't smile back.

"And with all your experience, you believe you're the one to give that to them?"

Blood rushed to her cheeks as his dull eyes stared at her. What was with his tone? Was he being sarcastic? She couldn't work it out.

"Pardon?"

"The solicitors at Eleanor's House are meant to be either extremely experienced or have had their own history of domestic violence. I don't believe you've had either."

Her mouth fell open as his words hit her like a slap to the face. Had he just said she didn't suit the job that she loved? That she sacrificed every spare minute for?

You've got to be kidding me.

Silence rained around them as more people joined their group, breaths baited as they waited for her response. She bit the inside of her cheek and inhaled through her nose as she weighed her words carefully. All preconceived notions about Nathan Johnson were mentally picked up and thrown out the window.

He was no longer her crush, nor her hero. He was the one with the power to take away the job she loved so much and gave her life purpose. In short, he was now the most important person in the world.

"No, you're correct. I'm neither."

Emily tilted up her chin and watched a coldness creep over Nate's beautiful blue eyes as that fake smile lifted up his lips. She didn't know who she'd met in the foyer, but this was not him.

"Well that's great for you, but I don't understand why you are working at the center. Perhaps I need to speak to the staff there about their hiring protocols since the standards seem to be slipping."

Oh no, no, no!

Emily froze, the bottom falling out of her life.

Kristy jumped to her defense. "Mr. Johnson, my associate graduated at the very top of her class and is one of the best solicitors they have at Coote and Douglas."

Nate's eyes travelled over to Kristy, his spine straightening to his full height of over six feet two or three. The simple, dominant move made his presence even more hugely felt.

"Then I am honored she is volunteering her time in the center, but I still don't think she is right for the women there."

He tipped his pretend hat in mock thanks to her and her jaw clenched, her belly tight. Cold rippled over her body until there was a sour taste in her mouth.

What was this shit?

Fuck not being personal.

How had he gone from being a beautiful gentleman to her one minute, and then this ruthless businessman?

"Nate, why are you being so rude all of a sudden?"

His eyes narrowed and the people around her continued to stare, their eyes boring into her with the weight of heavy fists. She didn't look away from his flint gaze, her anger giving her a strength that was foolhardy.

"Rude? I'm here to raise money and for no other reason. I've thanked you for your paltry contribution, what else do you want, Emily?"

What else do I want? You're fucking kidding me!

"Have you two met before?" Kristy's voice rose high around them and they broke off their visual battle to stare at Kristy.

Nate cocked his head. "Pardon?"

"You called her Emily and no one introduced her. Plus, she called you Nate."

Emily crossed her arms over her chest and pursed her lips together, a shiver wracking her once overheated frame. She wasn't answering that question.

"We met out in the foyer for a moment."

You mean I met Dr. Jekyll. You must be his evil twin.

"Oh."

Kristy nodded and stepped closer to her, sliding her hand into the crook of Emily's elbow. Kristy tugged at her so Emily let her arms drop, her friend pressing herself against Emily in a beautiful show of support.

Emily's jaw clenched into place as anger pooled in her gut like a lead weight.

"We both love working at the center, Mr. Johnson and admire what you've done to give women who are in dire straits a place they can call home for a short amount of time."

Emily nodded to agree with her friend, tugging up her lips in a semblance of a smile. She may be so confused she could barely speak, but that didn't change the fact that no matter what sort of guy Nathan Johnson was in real life, his work with Eleanor's House was incredible. Her mind whirled with all sorts of questions. What had happened to the man she'd seen out in the foyer? The gentleman who'd been kind and thoughtful and *genuine*? Why was he suddenly attacking her? Her lack of experience couldn't possibly be such a concern in a volunteer environment? She had to speak up.

"I love it too, Mr. Johnson, and hope you will rethink your position on me working there. There is nowhere I'd rather volunteer my time and would do anything for the women who stay there."

Was this all just an act? Even the kindness he showed the women she cared for? Pain rolled in her belly, clenching down.

I'm going to be sick!

"We better keep moving, Nathan. Lots more handshaking to do."

The blonde, who Emily had barely noticed standing there, spoke directly to Nate and he nodded, heading off to the next group without even a glance back in her direction.

Emily turned away and swallowed hard, putting a hand to her mouth to keep herself from screaming out loud.

"You look like you're about to internally combust. Let's go stand over there."

Emily allowed herself to be dragged to the corner where the food was. She picked up a cream puff and stuffed it into her mouth. She chomped on it and swallowed it down.

"What happened, Em?"

She pointed to Nathan Johnson, a man that up until five minutes ago, she'd admired with everything she had inside of her. How wrong could she be about a person? She should have known better than to be swayed by a handsome face and pretty manners. Ugh, she was disgusted with herself, too.

"Do you see him? Just look at him."

Kristy glanced that way and shrugged. "Yeah, so?"

Her stomach rolled but she forced herself to take some steadying breaths. She couldn't seem to get control of her breathing. He was only one man, but he had the power to take away something she held so dear to her heart. She couldn't let that happen.

"I thought Nathan Johnson was a philanthropist. A good man who believed in doing the right thing, for the right reason. But he practically told me I wasn't good enough to work at his charity and now he's schmoozing all those rich people for their money when they've never even set foot in the place before! If the reason he set up Eleanor's House was for the power, then I think I better find a new charity to start supporting."

She was properly panting now and she could barely stop herself from screaming aloud. Kristy gasped and poked her in the ribs, the sharp pain making Emily step back and glare at her friend.

"Hey!"

"You don't mean that! Pro bono work is your life."

Emily frowned and crossed her arms over her chest. "No, it's not." She had lots more in her life than that, especially her responsibilities to her mum. That was the number one priority and as long as she kept that going well, she'd be fine.

"Yes it is, and you know it. You do seventy-hour weeks at your job and then volunteer all weekend. I haven't seen you do anything else in two years and even before then you were bugging me to volunteer. Just because the guy who pays the bills is a jackass," Kristy waved her hand in the direction where Nate was still kissing people who had too much money, "does not mean you stop doing what you love."

Hot tears stung the backs of her eyes and Emily blinked rapidly. Nausea roiled in her belly and she grabbed a chocolate dipped strawberry, biting into it to stem the tide of tears. She was livid.

"I... but..." she took a deep breath, the air shuddering through her chest as she exhaled once again. No words would do justice to the emotions rolling through her at this moment, and Kristy didn't need to know her long sob story. "You're right. I love my work there and I can't let a prick like him stop me from doing what makes me happy." And it did. Volunteering at Eleanor's House lessened the guilt she felt about not being able to help her mother when she was younger, and it paved the way to a better future. She slept well at night knowing the world was a better place because of her.

"So if that means kissing his ass to keep your position, you'll do it?"

Emily huffed and let a soft laugh escape her. She wasn't sure she'd go that far, but she'd definitely fight for what she needed.

"Maybe a little."

Kristy threw her head back and laughed, then grabbed a pretty looking hors d'oeuvre. "That's the spirit. Now, who shall we meet next?"

2

Nate chuckled and lifted a glass of water from the silver tray the waiter carried.

"You're too generous, Mrs. Thomas. Thank you very much."

The old crone's wrinkled cheeks glowed beneath the praise and she handed him a check from her silver purse.

He took it and passed it directly to Martine, his executive assistant and the most organized woman he'd ever hired. "I'll make sure to put the receipt in the mail."

After all, the main reason most of these people donated money was for the tax benefits and that didn't bother him one whit, as long as they kept giving their money to *his charity*.

"You really are a saint, Nathan Johnson. Of all the things in the world to raise money for, domestic violence against women is so out of your orbit."

Nate grimaced out a smile and thanked the woman again, moving on to the next couple and the *next couple*. Endless chatter, thanks and smiles.

"Almost there, Nathan. One more thing to do and then you're done." Martine's voice in his ear made him straighten up to his full height, the heaviness on his shoulders lifting with her words.

He approached the stage and stepped up to the podium, the band quieting down on a descending scale until they were impossible to hear. The crowd in the room stopped talking, turning towards him *en masse.*

His heart clenched in his chest as he pulled out the prepared speech he'd written from the inside of his jacket, his other hand going into his pocket to search out the safety pin he kept there.

Empty. Bugger. That woman.

He bit his bottom lip and focused on the words written on the cards in front of him. Soon he would be able to support Eleanor's House one hundred percent. No more need for nights like this.

"Thank you, everyone, for coming this evening, and for your generous contributions to Eleanor's House. I will personally make sure that every cent raised here tonight goes towards the housing, food, counselling, child care, financial support, legal aid and job assistance that the women we help need."

He paused and a round of applause followed.

His eyes strayed away from the jewels and furs on the women in front of the stage to a single woman at the back of the room, her black dress being held up by one of his safety pins.

Emily's arms were crossed and her eyes blazed in her head, yet even with the straight lips and lifted chin, she was still charmingly beautiful. She had a great body for a short-term lover and he was in need of something new.

"I must leave shortly for the airport, but please continue bidding on our silent auction items and I will personally notify all the winners on Monday. Until then, thank you again for your support and I hope to see you all again next year."

The applause was louder this time and as he stepped off the stage, Martine wrapped her hand around his elbow and gently guided him towards the exit as she always did.

"Well done, although you could have said more."

Hardly necessary.

"I don't think so. I'm known for my short speeches."

They stepped up to the exit and Martine pulled him to a stop, tugging on his tie as she always did. He wasn't sure if she saw herself as a friend, an employee or his honorary sister sometimes. "You could always say something personal you know, so people don't think you're such a pompous ass."

Nate reached out and squeezed her chin, moving her face from side to side. "Now why on Earth would I do something like that?"

"Oh, because then that gorgeous little solicitor wouldn't have been giving you the death stare."

Nate's gut tightened and he turned around, assuming from Martine's tone that he would see Emily standing there behind him. But when he saw nobody relevant, he turned back to his assistant.

"And again, why would I want to do that?"

Martine crossed her arms over her chest, her bright green eyes challenging him to answer. "You went to a lot of trouble to piss her off, Nathan. Any particular reason?"

One of the waiters came by with his briefcase and coat, which he took with both hands. "You mean other than the fact that she's not qualified to volunteer at the center and she's some do-gooder that hasn't known a minute's trauma in her whole life?"

He grimaced and rolled his neck, a feeling of dirty water washing over him, making him shudder. When he'd first seen Emily out in the foyer he'd had an instant response to her, an unusual one, actually. Rather than just assessing her looks and seeing how quickly he could lure her into bed, he'd enjoyed her smile. Only one other woman had affected him in a similar way, and that affair had turned into the most dangerous of his life. He'd never put himself in a situation like that again. A woman such as she was poison to a man like him.

He'd known he'd have to find a way to separate himself from her so that he didn't fall for her obvious charms. When he'd found out she wasn't a young heiress and instead a pro bono solicitor, his belly had twisted inside him like she'd thrust a knife in his guts. Women like that were not meant for him. He couldn't trust himself around them, and they were too nice to be hurt by him.

He'd done the right thing. Better to cut her off early.

"Yeah, I know who she is Nathan, but you usually take advantage first. Take 'em home and then at least have the decency to send them on their merry way in a taxi. You didn't give this one the time of day unless I missed something and you managed a quickie in a coat closet? Ah, I didn't mean that." Martine held her hands up and chuckled as she stepped back.

Nate unlocked the clamp on his jaw and growled away some of the anger vibrating through his bloodstream. Emily wasn't that sort of girl and Martine should know that.

"No. I haven't had her, Martine. Only met her for a minute."

"Then what's with the prick mode and then the overreaction?" She frowned and scanned his face. He looked away. He paid Martine well because she was so adept at reading him, but the woman was far too perceptive for his own good sometimes.

He lifted his gaze and glared down his nose at his diminutive assistant.

"What's with the third degree, Martine? Since when do you care how I treat women?"

"Emily Sanders isn't exactly any woman, Nathan."

He put his briefcase down and pulled on his suit jacket. "What do you know about her?"

"I know everything, you know that."

Nate stared at her long and hard. He had little sway over this tiny female, but just trying was usually enough to get what he wanted.

She grinned and relented with a wink he knew too well. She was enjoying this.

"She's a saint, really. She's from a lower class background, no boyfriend, single mother family. She works hard, got amazing grades at University, and spends every spare minute she has in some charity or another."

Then his instincts had been on the money. A bloody saint with a passion that would rouse the worst in him.

"Like Eleanor's House, I suppose?"

"Yes. The supervisor there said she's unstoppable when it comes to getting the best outcome on her cases."

I don't want her around. I don't care how good a solicitor she is.

"She doesn't suit the center. You know I prefer people with personal experience working there."

Martine continued as though he hadn't spoken, "She's kind and most of all, she brings a ray of sunshine into their lives. Oh…"

Her mouth dropped open and Nate busied himself with straightening his coat and picking up his briefcase once again.

Yeah, she's perfect. I know.

"Oh, what Martine?"

"That's the problem isn't it? She's too good for you?"

He tossed his head and lifted his chin.

Not bloody likely.

"Nobody's too good for me. Didn't you see me in Australia's Most Eligible Bachelors?" True, he'd been right down the bottom of the list, thanks to the fact he wasn't uber-rich, but it hadn't stopped over a dozen women calling him this week alone.

She pushed him in the shoulder, her sharp nails digging into his skin even through the three layers of material. "You know that's not what I mean, Nathan. She's too innocent for you, isn't she? Too nice. I'm sure that isn't a problem you've come across before."

He rolled his eyes and changed the subject. This topic was growing tiresome.

"Yeah, something like that. Listen, email me the list of all the silent auctioneer winners and I want all the financials for the extension on the center to look at before Monday."

Martine nodded, tapping the silver clutch which held all of the checks for the night. "Will do. And your schedule on Monday has changed quite a bit, so go over it if you have time."

He nodded his thanks and moved out the door into the foyer, coming face to face once again with the little angel herself, her face flushed from heat or too much alcohol, he wasn't sure.

Her eyes widened when she saw him and he instinctively stopped.

"Good evening, Dr. Jekyll, I mean, Mr. Johnson. I do hope you let me stay on at Eleanor's House. You have created an incredible women's center there." She did a little curtsy and his stomach gripped tightly. God, she was beautiful. He'd never seen a warmth like she possessed shine from a woman.

Then her words sunk in and a reluctant smile spread over his mouth.

Dr. Jekyll? Oh, clever girl.

"I'll think about it, Emily. Good night, Ms. Sanders."

His voice came out a little harsher than he'd meant but she didn't falter, grinning at him as though she didn't care about the consequences. Her warm, brown eyes sparkled with mirth and she twirled a strand of dark hair around her finger, looking very similar to a teenager despite the elegant clothes and mature body.

She nodded and waltzed past him, literally dancing her way back into the ballroom.

A wave of longing passed over him like a heat wave in the middle of summer, prickling his skin and making his mouth run dry. He had spent his life running away from women like that. They needed so much more than he had to give, but there was something about her that just made him ache. If his rules weren't so firmly ingrained, he may have been tempted to try a date. Just one.

She's dangerous. Don't even think about it.

Nate clenched his teeth, tightly gripped his briefcase and marched straight out into the freezing cold night.

EMILY FELL into bed around midnight, her head spinning from far too much alcohol, and the balls of her feet throbbing from too much dancing. She'd spoken to so many incredible people and met the infamous Nathan Johnson himself. He may have threatened her pro bono work, the very glue that held her life together, but she'd spent the night convincing herself that she'd bring him around to seeing her side.

Everything would be all right.

Emily swatted the snooze button the next morning when the alarm blared at six am. She hated getting out of bed so early, but she had a few things to prepare for before she went to Eleanor's House to volunteer.

Her arms moved a little slower than usual as she got herself up and went about her normal morning routine. Despite her lethargy, her brain whirled through all the events of the night before at lightning speed. She still couldn't believe she'd fallen for the act that "Nate" had put on for her. She'd believed him to be a decent guy and then when she'd found out he was Nathan Johnson the philanthropist, she'd honestly thought the man of her dreams had arrived. But he'd turned out to be no better than a snobby elitist with no true care for those he helped at Eleanor's House.

She got dressed, ate breakfast and ventured out into the cold morning air with no one to be seen up and down her street. It took her old car five minutes to heat up until she could comfortably drive, and as she sat there shivering her butt off, she questioned her sanity about buying a house first, rather than a new car like all her friends had.

She grinned a little as she rubbed her hands together to stave off the chill, then slid the car into gear and took off. The luxury car would come later on. After she'd paid off her house and her mum's mortgage. When her mum had the financial security she deserved, Emily would start buying into the more extravagant side of life.

Emily parked outside Eleanor's House, locked her car and hurried inside, noticing it was chilly in there as well. She slid into her small office space and spread out, stretching her shoulders and back as the heater behind her roared to life.

Yay! Finally.

She looked up and smiled as Nicola, one of the other volunteers yawned loudly, her hands wrapped around an extra-large coffee cup as she strolled up. "I don't know how you always come in here so bright and bubbly Em. I feel like death warmed up without my caffeine in the morning." Emily smiled at the older woman. "I drink a lot of black tea, don't worry. What do we have today, Nic?"

Nicola's eyebrows rose high on her forehead, her tongue darting out to wet her lips. "Don't tell me you've already finished the cases I gave you last weekend?"

She pulled out some manila folders and pushed them across the desk in front of her. "Paperwork's all done. The McMillan child consent orders were lodged on Wednesday and I finally got a judge to sign off on Claudia's divorce on Friday."

That had been a pain in the ass. Claudia's husband and his prick of a solicitor had fought her every step of the way. But they'd gotten there eventually and Claudia would have a much better life now, without that scumbag dragging her down.

Frikkin' cheating, lying men.

Nicola took a long swallow of her coffee and shook her head.

"Don't you ever sleep, Em?"

She shrugged and looked away from her boss and towards her computer. Not when there was work to do and bad guys to put in their place, she didn't.

"Good morning, ladies."

Cindy, their supervisor, and the center manager bustled in, a cloud of floral perfume and hairspray enfolding her pretty features.

"Oh, Emily, great to see you. I have a new file for you this morning. An unusual one for this center actually but I'm hoping it will be right up your alley."

"That sounds intriguing."

"I need you to help me put together the contracts for the new extension that, thanks to the success of last night's ball, we can finally put into the works. I received an email this morning confirming permission for the proposed work. Which means we'll have two new offices and more than twenty new beds."

Cindy's face lit up like New Year's fireworks, the lines around her eyes deepening like sand under foot.

She mirrored her supervisor's happiness and grinned back.

"Oh, that's brilliant." As a corporate solicitor in her day job, juggling these sorts of contracts would be a piece of cake.

"You sure you don't mind the crossover? I mean, you do so much of this work during the week I don't want you to feel as though we're taking advantage of you."

She took the file and fluttered her hands at Cindy. "No way. This is great!"

Two more offices for volunteers and twenty new beds would be such a blessing for so many people. Emily knew that Cindy hated to turn people away to another shelter, but they reached capacity so often she barely had a day when she didn't have to.

"That's not all, Em. I need your help working on the ten-year anniversary celebration. It's next week and we totally forgot about it, but we can't just let it pass us by."

Emily gasped and shook her head. No way could they do that. It was a huge milestone.

"No, I agree. But what can I do other than help with the drinks and such?"

"You can help plan something special. We could bring some of our success stories back in to do a speech, put on a cocktail party maybe?"

"Brilliant idea." There were so many amazing women who had thrived because of the help they'd received here. It would be great to get them all together and talk about their success. "Yeah… absolutely. The more I think about it, the more I love it, Cindy."

Nicola sat on Emily's desk and addressed Cindy. "I heard from a friend that Emily really hit it off with Nathan Johnson last night at the fundraiser. Perhaps she could convince him to make a speech at the party too?"

Oh, you little bitch! Where did you hear that?

Cindy turned hopeful eyes on her, her mouth wide in shock. "Oh, Em! Do you really think you could? That would be amazing!"

Emily glared at Nicola but kept her smile in place for her supervisor. "Ah… I'm sure he'd be too busy on a Saturday night."

Cindy was practically fanning herself with excitement, her grin a mile wide. "Probably, but no one ever gets to see him or thank him personally for what he's done. Oh please, would you do it for me? I'd really appreciate it."

Emily cleared her throat and tried to inject a pleasant tone into her voice, but wasn't quite successful. Time with Nathan, begging him to speak about his achievements? She'd rather clean the toilet with her toothbrush. "Yeah, he's done so much…"

Cindy cocked her head and squinted at Emily. "I don't understand your tone."

Emily cleared her throat again and stood up so she wasn't the only one sitting. This conversation was going on longer than she'd anticipated. "Considering the man threatened to terminate my volunteer employment, I don't think I'm the best person for the job."

It was Cindy's turn to look aghast, her eyes widening and her mouth falling open. "You're joking. Why would he do that?"

Emily rolled her eyes. "Because he thinks I'm not experienced enough. He said everyone working here is supposed to have been abused themselves or be really experienced, and I'm neither."

Cindy chewed on her lip. "Well, that is true… but, I'll speak to them. We can't lose you, you're amazing!"

Emily considered Cindy's face and for the first time, *really* looked at her, seeing a gentle scar curving up between her nose and forehead and another along her hairline. She glanced away and cleared her throat.

Shit! I hadn't ever thought about what Cindy or Nicola might have gone through.

"Anyway, it doesn't matter. If he wants to get rid of me, there's nothing I can do to stop him." Even as she said it, the tears pooled in her eyes and she blinked them away. She'd find another charity, probably, but God she loved it here.

Time for a topic changer. "Back to the matter at hand. The party. I know he pays the bills around here, but he doesn't have anything to do with what goes on inside. Perhaps another speaker might be more…" She struggled to find any other word than *appropriate*, but considering the fact the man owned the building, it felt *inappropriate* to say so.

"You know he named this building after his mum, right?"

"No. Why would he do that?"

She'd never really thought about the name of Eleanor's House, which seemed kind of ridiculous now. Why hadn't she taken that into consideration?

Cindy shrugged. "I'm not one hundred per cent sure. There's a rumor that she was a victim of domestic violence herself, but no one really knows. Nathan Johnson and his past are a huge mystery."

A coldness dropped into the pit of Emily's belly and she swallowed hard. His mum? She couldn't even imagine something like that happening to her own beloved mother. No, she didn't want to be wrong about him again!

Bugger.

Nicola nodded, joining in the conversation once again. "That makes sense really. No man, no matter how wealthy, puts all his efforts into a women's charity unless it's personal."

Emily looked away, anger swirling in her belly like a summer storm, round and around.

"But you should have seen him last night. Schmoozing and kissing all those women for the money, which he doesn't even need! He's a billionaire in his own right. Do you seriously think he does it for the women who come through here and not the applause he receives for pretending to care?"

Nicola frowned, chewing on her lip for a moment. "You may have misjudged him, Em."

She stuck her nose in the air, determined to stick to her guns. After the way he'd treated her she didn't doubt her assessment for a minute.

The more she thought about it, the more she was convinced she was right. If he actually cared about the women in Eleanor's House, wouldn't he be in here helping, offering encouragement? Anything to show he cared.

"I doubt that very much." She was so rarely wrong about people.

Cindy glanced from Emily to Nicola. Her forehead creased with a frown but she didn't say anything else about Nathan Johnson. "So you'll do it? You'll at least ask him?"

Emily crossed her arms over her chest and considered her options. She didn't really have a choice, did she? She forced a smile to her face and some cheer into her voice. "I'll definitely try. But I'll help with the party no matter what he says. We'll make it an awesome celebration."

Knock, knock, knock.

"Emily!"

It was Claudia, one of the many clients she'd helped through her work at Eleanor's House, and although she didn't like to play favorites, this woman had definitely touched her heart more than most.

"Hey, Claudia, how are you?"

Emily smiled at Nicola and Cindy and walked out of her office to join the tiny woman who still wore the scars of her abusive husband across her eyebrows and cheekbones.

"I'm doing better thanks to everyone here. My, ah…"

"Ex-husband?"

A nervous giggle made it out of the tiny woman's mouth. "Yeah, I still can't believe you got him to sign the papers."

Emily shrugged and gave her lovely client a warm smile. These moments made every second she spent in the corporate jungle worthwhile.

"Magic happens sometimes, especially when karma lends a hand."

Big, soulful eyes stared up at her. "What do you mean?"

She reached out and gripped Claudia's hand, wishing she could will some strength into this lovely person. "I mean that you are a beautiful woman who deserves to be safe and happy."

"I am now. And it's all because of you, Emily."

Tears welled in Claudia's eyes and Emily laughed softly to distract herself from the hot lump in her throat. If she thought for one moment what Claudia's life would have been like without the support of everyone at Eleanor's House, she'd be in tears too.

She pulled Claudia into her arms, the woman's ribs protruding through her jumper beneath Emily's palms. Next stop was the nutritionist and getting some weight back onto her bones.

"Oh, you're so gorgeous. Thank you, but I think Cindy, Martha and Eleanor did a lot more than me."

Her heart swelled as she stood there for a moment and held Claudia. This was the reward for all of those hours she logged, unpaid and in her free time. It may not help pay off her mortgage any faster, but she felt more appreciated at this job than she did in any other avenue of her life.

WHEN SHE ARRIVED home that night, Emily turned on all the lights, locked the door and collapsed onto her second-hand couch. It may be worn at the edges and a bit shabby by some people's standards, but it was hers, and it was comfortable.

She groaned and let her head fall back against the soft headrest, her throbbing scalp making her eyes slide closed. The relief the darkness gave her was small, but welcome.

Ring, ring, ring.

"Argh! Five minutes, I just need five minutes."

She heaved herself up off the couch and rummaged through her bag to pull out her phone.

She glanced at the screen, swiped it open and answered with a sigh. "Hey, Mum."

"Hello, my beautiful daughter. How have you been?"

She settled back into the couch, the leather soft beneath her back. "Good. Busy. Work, mostly."

"Of course, you've been working. You do nothing but work."

Emily threw her hands up in the air. "Muuum."

"Don't get me wrong, Em. I am so proud of you, but there is so much more to life than work."

She put her hand to her head and let her eyes close again. Same conversation, same topic. "I know."

But what are we supposed to do for money if I don't work? And do you seriously think I want to be in a situation where the bank can just take my house and yours too, if they want? No.

"Then why aren't you out enjoying yourself? Going out with friends, dating young men?"

Because young men are stupid and I don't have time.

"I do go out. In fact, I went to a charity ball last night."

"That's lovely honey, but I'm sure it was related to your work."

A groan escaped her and she shuffled around so that she was lying down on the couch, her tired feet coming up to rest on the cushions. She loved her mum to bits, but a little bit of gratitude occasionally would be nice. "It was, but I danced, I drank champagne, it was awesome."

A moment of shocked silence and then her mum chuckled a little. "That's so great, Em. So when am I seeing you next?"

Emily lifted her neck and pulled the hair elastic out of her ponytail. She gasped with the stretching pain and then the relief as she let her head fall back onto the couch cushion and the tension drained out of her. "Whenever you want. I work until ten most nights and all weekend. Do you do midnight runs?"

Her mother laughed properly this time, the deep sound vibrating down the phone line. "I love you."

A familiar warmth spread through her and she smiled to herself. "I love you too, Mum."

"Do you promise to try to make some time for me? I know it's a couple of hours drive to my place from the city, but even if you have to invite me to one of those charity events. I'll pay to see you."

Her smile turned to a frown as she assessed everything her mum was saying. She rarely left the comfort of her town and sewing circle. As for the money, she'd happily pay for her mum to come visit her, but would she?

"Well actually, I'm organizing a celebration for Eleanor's House. I don't think you'll have to pay, but can I let you know closer to the day and you might want to come?"

She didn't want to get her hopes up, especially considering how long it had been since she'd seen her mother.

"I would love that, sweetie. I'll just have to check my calendar and get back to you."

"Thanks." Her throat caught a little which she didn't mean to have happen and she swallowed hard. Her mother had suffered from fibromyalgia most of her life, and she struggled to travel. Her anxiety didn't help either.

She won't come.

"Of course. See you soon."

Her mum had raised her alone after her dad's business had fallen apart and he'd run off with some woman. Her life hadn't been easy and she deserved so much more than her current quiet existence.

Emily let her eyes close and her fingers linked together over her belly as her muscles turned to liquid. Just a few more years and they'd be free.

3

$\mathcal{E}$mily's eyes flicked from paper to screen and back again. Her head pounded a little but she was focused. Her caseload was full which was stressful, but she loved the mental stimulation of her job.

An email arrived that caught her eye and Emily opened it, her eyebrows climbing her forehead until she felt the creases press up against her hairline.

Dear Emily Sanders,

Johnson Property Development requests your attendance at a meeting at 1 p.m. today.

Please confirm

Kind Regards,

Martine Nichols

Nathan Johnson's Executive Assistant.

Wow. What do they want? Oh, no! Not my job.

Emily clicked reply and held her hands poised over the keyboard. She had no idea what to write, her mind had gone from having ten screens operational to one blank canvas. What if Nathan Johnson was following through with his threat to get her out of Eleanor's House?

Her stomach tightened as her hands shook. She reached for the phone, squinted at the screen and typed in the number at the bottom of the email. She shouldn't jump to conclusions. She had questions, so the most logical thing to do was ask.

The phone rang and Emily straightened her spine, taking a deep breath to calm her galloping heart. If she lost Eleanor's House, she'd find another charity.

"Martine Nichols."

The blonde from Saturday night perhaps?

"This is Emily Sanders. I just received an email regarding an appointment this afternoon." *And I have no idea what it is about.*

"Ah, yes. Great. You're confirming the time?"

Oh, no...

Emily picked up a pen and began tapping it against the wooden desk. "Ah, I was actually wondering what the appointment is regarding?"

She dropped the pen and inhaled until her lungs were full to bursting. Were they setting up a meeting to fire her?

"Martine, if this is about Saturday night..."

"We would like to hire you for some contract work."

What?

Emily exhaled the breath she had been holding and stared at her computer screen with unseeing eyes. Her heart rate that had taken off at light speed when she'd thought she was about to lose her volunteer position, was now thumping with sickening precision against her sternum.

Thank goodness for that.

"All right. But may I ask why haven't you made an appointment to come to my office?"

Which would be normal procedure considering she would need to be hired through her own firm.

"I spoke to the senior partner there this morning and explained our need to have you onsite for a day or two. He seemed fine with that and suggested I contact you directly."

Hmm... of course he would. James Allen knew how much work she could get done and he enjoyed making sure her load was as full as possible. So she didn't really have any choice, did she?

"Of course, now the time for today was?"

The rest of the conversation passed and Emily got back to her work. Her gut had tightened in a sign of bad things to come, and she trusted her instincts more than anything.

"Hello, I'm Martine, Mr. Johnson's Executive Assistant."

Emily held out her hand and tried not to let her eyes roam over the beautiful woman in front of her. It was rude and she hated it when people did it to her, but Martine was gorgeous. She *was* the same woman who'd been in the red dress on Saturday night, but in her corporate attire she was even more breathtaking than in formal wear.

Her minimal makeup accentuated her flawless skin and huge eyes, while the designer black skirt and suit jacket accentuated her femininity without making her sexually aggressive. An amazing ensemble and one Emily wished she could emulate.

"It's nice to see you again, Martine. I'm Emily Sanders."

"Thank you so much for coming in on such short notice. Emily. Please take a seat."

Emily sat on the black leather chair facing Martine and glanced around the small room. Whose assistant had her own office? Or was she more than just an E.A?

"I'll get straight to the point, Emily. We need a new solicitor for our team and we would like you to join us in representing our company. You were highly recommended and with our constant expansion, we always need good corporate solicitors on our side."

Emily blinked in confusion and waited for all the words to sink in. Working for Nathan Johnson? Really?

"That is a huge compliment, thank you, but who recommended me?"

"Cindy from Eleanor's House."

Emily blinked again. That was lovely of her, but a little unexpected. Or was it? Cindy said she'd fix the problem of her working at the center, but she hadn't expected more corporate work from it. "I'll have to remember to thank her. There are so many amazing solicitors who work at Eleanor's House."

Actually, there were a couple that rotated around. Emily was the only one who'd worked there with any regularity over the past two years.

"Emily, you are a stand-out in both of your jobs and that's why we're offering you our new accounts section."

Emily sat up straighter in her chair, feeling under-briefed and ill-prepared. She hardly knew anything about Nathan Johnson's company and as she wiggled in her chair, she felt unworthy of the praise being heaped on her.

"I'm sorry. I don't quite understand. On Saturday night Nate literally told me he didn't want me working at Eleanor's House at all, and now he wants me working here?"

Martine smiled at her, the gesture lighting up her already pretty face.

"I do all the hiring in our company and I believe you are perfect for the position. As far as Eleanor's House is concerned, you'll need to sort it out with Mr. Johnson and Cindy."

Emily nodded once.

Message received loud and clear.

Nate wasn't the one hiring her and she still needed to deal with the issue of her "inexperience" with the boss man.

Time to get down to business.

"What sort of hours would you require of me? I'm pretty flat out at the moment, but of course I'd love to take you on as a client if it is possible."

She took out her daily planner and notebook, her head spinning with the speed at which this was happening. But behind the panic there was a lot of happiness building. This would be the first client she'd independently brought into the firm and her supervisor would be delighted. Climbing the corporate ladder was hard, especially for a woman, and any help she got along the way was a bonus.

An abrupt knock sounded on the door and then it opened. She turned towards the intruder, a dark haired man stepping into the small space of Martine's office.

Emily's pulse quickened as her eyes took in the tailored suit, strong, straight back and intense blue eyes of the one she'd called Nate.

"Mr. Johnson, it's nice to see you again."

His head turned towards her, his gaze like flint as his mouth thinned into a straight line. "Emily."

She raised her eyebrows as she stood up and faced him. *Really?*

"Oh, are we on a first name basis again, Mr. Johnson?"

Be careful! You still need to ask him not to fire you from Eleanor's House.

"I don't see why not, Emily."

She crossed her arms and lifted a hand, tapping her finger against her lip as heat bubbled in her belly. She shouldn't goad him—she knew she shouldn't—but he was standing there all cold and perfect and a part of her wanted to reach out and pull his pristine blue tie off center.

"Well, I do see a couple of reasons why not. I'm confused as to whom I am speaking, for starters. Are you Nathan at the moment? Or Mr. Johnson? Because I'm pretty sure Nate hasn't appeared again?"

Martine cleared her throat and Emily unlocked her gaze, glancing back towards her.

Shit, I totally forgot she was still in the room.

Martine's gaze dropped down at her feet and began edging towards the door. "I'm going to pop out to the copier for a moment. I left the contracts there. Be back in a minute."

She shuffled out of the room and Emily went back to glaring at the man she'd soon call her boss. Lightning blue shot through his once cold eyes as electricity crackled in the air.

Emily broke off her stare to pick up her bag and rustle through it. She'd been carrying the stupid thing for days. She yanked open the side pocket and pulled out the safety pin she'd carefully tucked away. The metal was cold in her fingertips as she held it out to him.

"Here you go."

Nathan stared at her hand for a moment and then a grin broke out on his face like the sun emerging from a storm cloud, the darkness dissipating for pure light and beauty to emerge.

Her hand trembled as the anger drained from her body. He'd changed back into the man she'd met in the foyer. Nate.

Crap.

He reached into his own pocket and pulled out another, identical safety pin.

"Got one, thanks. You should keep that one in case of emergencies."

A smile quivered on her mouth and she licked her lips while palming the safety pin and tucking it back into her bag.

"Why on earth would you carry a safety pin around in your pocket all the time?"

Darkness crossed over his face like the shadow of death in biblical times, and her belly clenched tight in fear of what he was about to say. Then his eyes cleared and he cocked his head at her with a cheeky grin.

"You never know when a damsel in distress will need saving."

She couldn't stop the giggle that emerged. If he hadn't stepped on her dress, she wouldn't have needed saving, of course, but that was not a line of conversation she wanted to pursue at the moment. She wanted to know more about him.

"Oh, and you're the man for the job, is that right? You really do have a knight in shining armor complex, don't you?"

He turned his head away and a muscle ticked in his jaw, her arrow obviously finding a target in him. It made perfect sense if Cindy and Kristy were right about him. Why the cold businessman exterior, then?

When he finally looked back at her for a moment, something twisted inside her chest, making her gasp and glance at the dark carpet.

Martine bustled back in, her slight figure making quite an impact in the small room. "So, did you have time to speak about the terms of the contract?"

"Contract?"

"For your employment."

Emily opened her mouth to rebut the assumption being made, but there really wasn't anything to discuss. She couldn't turn down a client of this magnitude and since they'd already gone to the senior partner, she didn't have a choice.

"I would assume they are pretty standard?"

Martine nodded and smiled at her. She reached out a hand and Martine neatly slid the papers into her open grasp.

"Yes, but I'm sure you'll look over everything yourself."

Of course I will.

Emily dropped the papers into her black briefcase, her head spinning from the speed in which Martine organized everything. No wonder Nathan's business was in such good working order.

She considered the cute little blonde and the dark hunk at her side and spent a moment wondering if they were sleeping together. Martine had been affectionate and quite familiar at the ball the other night and the thought had crossed her mind then, but there was no warmth between them now.

She cocked her head again. It would be pretty stupid to sleep with your assistant, but then again, when it came to their dicks, men weren't known for being terribly smart.

"Welcome to the company, Emily, I will be seeing you at a later date, I'm sure." Nathan moved towards the door and Emily took a few quick steps towards him. She may as well ask the question now.

"May I speak to you for a moment, Mr. Johnson?"

He lifted his hand and indicated she should follow him. "I have a few minutes before my next meeting."

Emily kept pace with his long legs, following him down the brightly lit hall and stepping into a large corner office with huge windows overlooking the city.

Wow! Look at that.

"What was it in regards to?"

"Um…" Emily pulled her eyes away from the silver skyscrapers and colorful art out the window and shook her head. *Concentrate.* "I need to talk to you about Eleanor's House, actually." She had two things to ask now that she thought about it. "Number one, of course, is the issue of me not being experienced enough to work at the center. But I guarantee you, Mr. Johnson, that I have logged more hours in the past few years than most solicitors of my age. I am more than qualified to do the work that needs to be done."

He tapped his fingers together. "It's not just your technical skills that I'm concerned about. It is a firm belief of mine that only people that have been in that situation themselves can really advise people on those very personal topics. I appreciate the fact that you're a good solicitor Emily, that is obviously why Martine has asked you to come work for us, but at Eleanor's House there needs to be more than a good brain behind the people who work there."

Emily clenched her fingers into fists and stared at the ground, heat flushing up her cheeks in an uncomfortable blush. She did have experience in the field, although unfortunately not the sort that he had asked about.

"I do have experience that helps these women. I'm not very comfortable talking to people about it."

"Then please sit down."

His commanding tone had her dropping into the seat opposite him and looking up to meet his calm gaze.

"I generally have full hiring and firing power at the center, or did until Cindy took over. But she has done such a good job of running the place, she's also taken over that role. I always made sure the volunteers were suitable for the position."

Wow, she hadn't realized he'd had such a hand in its undertaking before now. She shouldn't have jumped to conclusions quite so fast.

"So you want me to share some of my past with you?"

She gulped down the lump in her throat as he nodded.

"Yes please, if you wish to continue to volunteer at Eleanor's House."

Her back straightened as determination set in. Was that a threat? Well, then fine, she wasn't afraid of him.

"My parents lost their home and their business and had to declare bankruptcy when I was eleven. My father ran off with some other woman and my mother raised me by herself."

Her new employer blinked and sat up straighter in his chair. "And that makes it easier for you to relate to the women at the center?"

"Yes, it does. These women often have had their homes ripped away from them and their children. They feel powerless and hopeless, just as my mother did, and I am determined to make sure that doesn't continue to happen, not on my watch."

Nathan glanced down and picked up a ballpoint, staring at it as though it held the key to the universe. "Then you may continue to volunteer at Eleanor's House. Thank you for your time."

Emily's shoulders dropped as a wave of cool relief washed over her.

"Thank you. It really does give me such a sense of purpose."

As she rose she heard him say under his breath, "Yeah, me too."

Which reminded her—the party.

"Oh, I have one more thing to ask you. On Saturday, we're having the anniversary celebration for Eleanor's House. We're considering holding a cocktail party and inviting clients from the past ten years to attend. We were also hoping to have a few key speakers, including yourself."

Nathan looked up at her and then away again, a muscle tightening in his jaw as he made a dismissive gesture with his hand.

"Please email me about that, Emily. I don't mix business with pleasure."

He turned his back to her, spinning his chair away so that she could no longer see him. If that wasn't the most obvious expression of shutting someone out, she didn't know what was.

She took a step closer to his desk and bit her lip as tension shivered through her. What sort of button had she pressed there?

She frowned at him and weighed her words carefully. There was something special about this man that made her want to connect with him, whether it was due to their mutual obsession with Eleanor's House or a similar past, she wasn't sure. But she wanted to find out. "I would have assumed a decision about Eleanor's House was all business."

He spun around to face her, his eyebrows drawn together and that flint gaze back in his blue eyes.

"Why would you say that?"

She shrugged and swallowed hard. His eyes were pretty intense when they were focused on her. "It certainly looked like it the other night."

"No. Eleanor's House is personal and I believe I have already indicated that."

"Well no, you indicated that you ran the charity like any good manager would, but I assumed it was still just a business to you."

She couldn't help baiting him a little bit longer. She loved a good puzzle and he was like one of those 3D Rubik's cubes that every time you moved one line, something else would stuff up the last move.

"Well, you're wrong."

"It's a tax deduction is it not, Mr. Johnson?"

Again that muscle ticked in his jaw and his gorgeous, thick lips pulled into a thin line. "It is."

She cocked an eyebrow at him. "Then how is that personal?"

His eyes blazed at her and her conscience nagged at her for being antagonistic. She had the strangest feeling that she was baiting a bear with a sore paw but she couldn't help it. He'd forced her to reveal something very personal about herself and he wasn't doing anything to reciprocate.

Technically he could achieve a tax dodge on anything. Why pour money into a women's shelter?

"That is none of your business and if you say one more word on the topic, Ms. Sanders, I will call your employer and have you dismissed."

Lead dropped Emily's belly down and her mouth gaped.

"Please, sir, I'd ask you to reconsider."

Tears stung her eyes as she pleaded with him, the consequences of her pushing him now coming home to roost. Could she find another job quickly if it became a necessity? How far ahead was she on the mortgage? Her mum should be right for a while…

Oh, God!

Nathan stood up slowly, tugged down hard on his jacket, then stepped around his desk and stalked forward like a powerful cat.

She gasped and backed up, lifting her hands up to ward him off. Nathan's nostrils flared and his fists clenched as he advanced on her.

Her spine pressed up against the plaster wall and he came within an inch of her chest, his breathing rapid and his gaze completely focused on her.

Her throat ached as she gulped hard and stared up into his intense blue eyes.

Something shifted in the charged atmosphere around them and Nathan's eyes became softer, his gaze dropping to stare at her lips.

Her mouth was parched and she nervously licked her lips, as Nathan's head bent towards her as though he was going to kiss her. She held her breath and didn't move, unable to do anything but wait for him as his lips came closer and closer to hers.

Emily's heart thumped against her ribs and she let out a small squeak.

Nathan pulled back and shook his head as though dazed.

"Excuse me."

He twisted and opened the door next to her, leaving the huge room and taking all the air and warmth with him.

Emily shivered and pressed herself against the wall as her knees shook and threatened to give way. She wrapped her arms around herself and swallowed the small sob that rose in her throat.

That had been close, too close. She couldn't let anything like that happen again.

She may be more attracted to him than she'd ever been to anyone in her life, but he now held all the cards, and if she wasn't careful her life would come tumbling down like those flimsy card towers she'd made as a girl.

Remove just one, and everything would come crashing down.

4

---

*N*ate tapped his fingers against his desk and stared at his computer screen, the numbers and figures of his latest design whirling around in a black and white blur.

"Bloody hell."

He threw himself back in his chair and stared up at the ceiling, his brain now free to wander to the subject of his desire...or obsession. He'd already spent too many hours engrossed by thoughts of her and that really needed to stop.

She was just a woman, and a solicitor at that. He ran a hand down his face and groaned.

The question he really wanted to be answered was, *why* did he find her so desirable? She was attractive, sure. But no more than every woman who worked on this floor. They were all thinner, too.

He grunted and rolled his eyes.

He didn't want thinner, he wanted those delicious curves, that easy smile, those beautifully polished nails. Which was another unusual thing about her. She was so untouched compared to all the other women he knew. Her hair seemed to be its natural color, her face rarely had more than a touch of mascara and her clothes were certainly nothing to write home about.

Why her, though? She was smart, yes. But many women he met were smart. She liked to probe him with rather deep questions, and that was a bit of a rarity. It had been a long time since someone had seemed genuinely curious about him. Reporters always asked the same questions and he barely answered them with any sort of civility.

But with Emily he wanted to share his secrets, which was a dangerous thing. Her obsession with his philanthropic side was probably the most refreshing development. Some of his past girlfriends had liked the idea on the surface, had oohed and ahhed about how kind he was, how thoughtful, how selfless. That was until it had affected what they could have, or how much time he could spend with them, let alone the fact that those women would practically pass out at the suggestion that they volunteer at his shelter, or do anything useful with their time.

Emily, on the other hand, spent every spare moment she had on the charity, and not just helping out, but using her very saleable skills to help women who would otherwise not have access to the assistance she offered.

And why was that?

"Yes."

He snapped his fingers and reached for the phone, an idea forming in his head.

He was being curious, that was all, about a new employee. He had every right to find out more about her.

He pressed a single button and the phone began to ring, which was quickly picked up on the other end by the woman of his literal daydreams.

"Hello, Emily speaking."

"Emily, it's Nathan Johnson. I have a few questions in regards to Eleanor's House and I was wondering if you would join me for dinner tonight to discuss them."

His belly plummeted to his feet in mortification and his mouth hung open. That was not what he'd planned to say at all. Why was he setting up a date with a woman who would not suit his life?

"Ah, I'm not sure that would be professional, Nathan."

She's giving you an out. Take it.

Not a chance.

"Of course it is. We both work too many hours a day anyway, so conducting a meeting while eating just kills two birds with one stone."

There was silence on the end of the line and he inhaled quickly through his nose. He didn't usually have to try with women, at all. Waiting like this was rather a novel experience.

"Nathan...I..."

She stopped and he jumped into the silence, knowing full well he was being stupid. Emily was bright and bubbly and passionate. She would pull out a side of him that he'd left behind fifteen years ago. But he'd already exposed his desire to see her, so he may as well put both feet in.

"You said you were interested in knowing more about Eleanor's House."

"You would answer some of my questions?"

Only if I want to.

He dropped the tone of his voice to sound playful. "You can't possibly have more questions, Emily?"

She responded to his tone with a gentle laugh. When the sound came through the phone it caused a strange clench and tightening in his chest.

"Oh, I always have questions Nathan, and I would love to know more about Eleanor's House."

Her happy vibe transmitted through the phone line and he found himself grinning. He exhaled a breath he hadn't realized he'd been holding. When she was being charming, all the reasons why he stayed away from women like her went straight out the eleventh-story window. "I have some questions of my own. You happy to answer some of mine?"

"There's not much to tell I'm afraid, but we don't need to speak about yesterday do we?"

Nathan swallowed a groan. His groin ached at the mere thought of the kiss they'd almost shared.

"No. Of course not, Emily."

He'd rather just repeat every single breath-stealing moment and change the ending. He still couldn't believe he'd almost kissed her. He'd sworn to himself not to even go near her and then he'd been pressing her up against the wall like some teenager who couldn't control himself.

A teenager…that was the reason he wouldn't be dating her. Because she made him behave like an unruly teenager! But if that were true, why had he stopped? Sure it would have been a monumentally stupid idea, but he regretted his control now. To taste her passion would be a new experience, he was certain.

He wasn't dating her anyway. He was having a dinner business meeting.

"So I'll pick you up at seven, shall I?"

"That's fine. I'll meet you out the front of my building, if you want. There're a few good restaurants close by."

"Good. See you then."

EMILY PULLED her handbag strap back to the top of her shoulder once again, the leather slipping down in the most annoying way.

I need a new one.

She groaned and turned to her left again, her eyes darting up and down the street. She hugged her arms closer to her body and shivered.

It was getting cold. Where was he?

"Emily."

She twisted around, her breath catching in her throat as Nathan Johnson stepped closer. His tie was missing, his top button undone atop a crisp white shirt. Her belly turned and her knees literally wobbled at the sight of him.

She cleared her throat and straightened her spine.

Stop being such a girl! And a stupid one, at that.

"Nathan."

"You can call me Nate, you know."

Uh, I don't think so.

She frowned and stared up at him. That would mean she'd have to forget about the other personalities that often made appearances and she wasn't sure she could do that at the moment. "I haven't heard anyone else call you Nate."

He shrugged and they began walking down the street together.

"Not at work, but outside I don't see why not."

She considered him for a moment, his relaxed stance and smile making her remember what he had been like the first night she'd met him. Against her own better judgement, she decided to give him the benefit of the doubt.

"Okay, Nate."

He grinned at her, truly *grinned,* and her heart fluttered in her chest. He had beautiful, straight white teeth and his blue eyes sparkled like sunshine on a dark pond. He appeared young and happy, an image she'd never seen in any interview photo or magazine article. Why was that? Why did he hide so much of himself?

"In here?"

She glanced at the ritzy restaurant he had indicated and shrugged. "Yeah, sure, why not? I've never tried it before."

Mostly because it looks expensive and I don't waste money on food. But then again, how often do I get to eat with a man who owns half the city?

He held open the glass door for her and she couldn't stop herself from grinning as she passed through the entrance and stepped into a whole new world.

Crisp, white tablecloths adorned the tables and tinkling classical background music played. The food here would be way out of her price range.

"This looks a bit fancy for a business dinner. You sure you don't want to keep walking?"

She was way out of her depth here. The whole restaurant was filled with couples canoodling and gorgeous women all done up to the nines.

A blonde at the table to her right stared at her, glanced up and down her body, sneered, then went back to her date, a man three times her age.

Emily tugged on her ill-fitting shirt sleeves. She still had her hair pulled up tightly in a bun and her off-the-rack suit did nothing for her figure, she knew that. But all her money went into the mortgages, she didn't waste money on labels.

She glanced again at Nate and sighed. His suit jacket probably cost more than most of her furniture combined. It was cut to perfection and obviously custom tailored.

"No. I like it. Let's sit."

She resisted rolling her eyes. *Of course you do.*

He spoke to the maître d' and they were escorted to a table in the back of the restaurant.

She sat down when the chair was pulled out for her, not quite sure how this had happened. One moment she'd been working too hard at her desk and now she was having dinner with one of the most eligible bachelors in the city and would also soon be working with him.

"I'm starving, shall we order?"

"Sounds like a plan."

She scanned the menu, quickly ordering a risotto that cost more than half her weekly grocery bill, but would keep her going until the morning. She had a big night of work ahead of her.

"So, tell me more about you, Emily."

She chuckled at his tactics. She wasn't interested in conducting this night like an interview or a rerun of some bad dating show.

"How about this—let's ask each other three questions and we have to answer with complete honesty."

She had no fear of what he'd ask her. Her life was boring and she preferred to be honest. Lying came badly to her and the few times she'd made mistakes in her life and lied about them later, the guilt had eaten away at her for months. On the flip side, though, she was very intrigued by the man in front of her. What was he hiding behind that obviously false mask?

His smile faltered and he shifted in his chair.

"I'm not sure I want to play this game, Emily."

"What's the problem, Nate? Scared?"

He grimaced out a smile and tugged at his cuffs like he was showing her he wasn't hiding any cards.

"Any three questions or must they be work related?"

To her, they were one and the same. "Anything's fine by me."

His blue eyes flashed with something hot at this idea and he sat up straighter.

"All right, I'll indulge you. The terms and conditions are set. Ladies first."

Emily opened her mouth, then snapped it shut again. If she wasn't a bit clever she'd blurt out the first thing that came into her mind and she wouldn't find out anything of real importance. She may be the solicitor, but he was a successful businessman and a bachelor. He wouldn't be trapped by any question very easily.

"Why is Eleanor's House personal to you?"

Nate blew out a long breath and placed both of his hands on the table, laying them palms down and pressing until his knuckles all but disappeared.

"You had to start with a hard one, didn't you?"

A laugh rose and escaped before she could stop it. "Technically I've already asked you this question, you just never got around to answering it properly."

He took a moment and then spoke, his tone smooth and deep.

"Eleanor's House is personal to me because I did it for no other reason than to give back to the community. Sure, my accountant finds a way to get a tax break from it, but if he couldn't, I'd still do it."

Emily cocked her head and stared at him. He didn't seem to be lying. There were no outwards signs of it, but was he aware that he hadn't even answered the question properly?

She didn't want to change the words of the request too much, in case he counted it as a second question, but she wanted a real answer. So she cleared her throat, used a stronger tone and rephrased it a little.

"That's very generous of you, but that doesn't have anything to do with being personal. Why is it personal to you, the charity?"

This time, he glanced away and ran a hand through his hair, ruffling the perfectly styled coif.

"Ah, I'm not sure I want to answer this one."

"Come on, I promise not to tell anyone."

He shrugged and lifted his chin, something strange transpiring behind his blue eyes. Whoever said that eyes were the windows to your soul had been right, but Nate had a damn good set of shades on his windows and it was going to take a crowbar to pry them open. "I set up Eleanor's House because my mother died from abuse."

Something cold and hard hit Emily in the gut and she gasped from the shock.

"I am so sorry." She reached across to the hand still lying on the table, lightly touching the warm skin of his knuckles. He pulled his hand away so quickly it made her stomach clench tightly once again.

Had he been abused too? Affection seemed to be a problem for him.

Oh God, Nate, I'm so, so, sorry.

She cleared her throat and averted her gaze. Now was not the time to ask such a thing.

She focused back on him, steering away from the subject as quickly as possible. "Your turn. Ask away."

"Why do you work so hard? What are you trying to achieve?"

She grinned at him. "That's two questions."

"Not really, I'm just leading you."

She smiled at his use of a good solicitor's trick but allowed him the freedom to do so. After being so honest with her, he deserved it.

"It's pretty simple, really. I want to do some good in the world. My parents had their house and business taken from them when I was young because they couldn't afford a decent solicitor who might have fought for them. They really struggled after that and I don't want to ever be in that situation again. It ripped my parents apart."

"So you want to make lots of money?"

She thought about that. Money itself wasn't the actual point, but what it gave her was important. "Not really. I want to be financially secure and independent, and now that I'm doing relatively well, I need to do more, too. I want to help people who can't help themselves. It makes me feel good."

"And you want to be the best?"

Definitions of that varied, so she decided to sidestep it as simply as possible. "Not exactly, but there is some satisfaction in being good at my job, too."

"Then we're kindred souls in that regard. Your turn again."

Now that was a telling statement if ever there was one, but she had suspected that herself. It seemed that both of them wanted to make up for the past in some way.

She chuckled and shook her head. That had been more like five questions, but again, she wasn't calling him on it. He was talking, sharing and exposing more of himself than he meant to. She wasn't stopping him now.

Their food arrived and Emily took a moment to inhale the sweet scent of parmesan, cream and garlic before biting her lip in hesitation.

Where could she lead him now?

"Tell me, why aren't you married?"

He laughed at that one, the sound a little harsh for her liking. "Simple really. I haven't met a woman I wanted to date for more than a month, let alone keep around for the rest of my life."

Oh goodness. What sort of women have you been sleeping with?

"Do you think so little of women in general?"

"No, but I must admit that the fantasy those romantic movies project is pretty far from the truth. I haven't met a woman yet who wasn't obsessed with money, looks, and status."

She swallowed the creamy forkful of risotto. "Well, you have now."

"I have what?"

"Met a woman not obsessed by any of those things."

His eyes roamed over her face with cynicism etched into his brow. She continued to stare at him as heat flowed up her face and bloomed across her cheeks. She didn't really like telling people too much about herself, but she wanted him to understand.

"I have an old car and an even older house, but they're mine. I try to make myself presentable but I think it's pretty obvious that I don't conform to fashion or the weight restrictions that are placed upon women."

And there was no way she was ever going to change. She loved rich food, her curves, and her old-fashioned values.

"And status, Emily? You don't want to snag yourself a wealthy husband who can fly you all over the world, present you at the most glamorous parties and give you everything your little heart desires?"

She laughed out loud at that one although it hurt her throat to do so. Part of her would love to be spoiled a little bit, who wouldn't? But marrying for money? Never.

She levelled her eyes at him.

"What my heart truly wants is a man who is kind, funny and hard-working. A man who appreciates me for who I am, not what I can give him and more than anything in the world, I want to feel that I am loved, every day. Always."

He sneered at her, although his hand shook a little as he reached for his glass. "I've heard such things sprouted at me before, but never so eloquently put, Emily." He lifted up his glass in mock salute and drank some of his water.

She tried her best to ignore the cheap shot and picked up her fork, forcing her hand to lift the food to her lips and eat it.

Her breathing rate had increased, as had her pulse. She was offended on behalf of every good woman she had ever met, but she needed to stay calm. Nathan Johnson would be hunted by every gold-digging woman in the country. He was allowed to be a little cynical.

"Your turn, Nate. Next question."

His face sobered and his lips flickered in a small smile, the most genuine look he'd given her all night. Something told her that he was impressed by her control, but as she forced her fingers to unwind from the fist they made under the table, she wasn't so happy with her lack of it.

"Tell me about the best sex you've ever had."

Emily's mouth literally dropped open. Thank goodness she hadn't been eating or drinking anything at that point in time.

"Umm." She had agreed to answer any question he asked, but she honestly hadn't expected such a thing. "I'm sure it would be extremely boring to you."

He tilted his chin up. "Try me."

HER LIPS WERE SO damn juicy, pink and lush, like a plum he just couldn't wait to taste. Nate couldn't drag his eyes away from them. He clenched his fingers into a fist on the top of the table and waited for her answer to his question.

She tapped her fingers on the table and drank her water, obviously trying to find a way around his question.

He'd been pretty blatant, but he had to find an angle around this woman. She was far too likeable, attractive and warm. He wasn't used to those sorts of females. Every girlfriend he'd ever had was at least fifty percent bitch. It was a reliable statistic that suited his world well.

Emily was just plain strange and intriguing.

"The best sex I ever had was my first time, actually."

"What?"

He sat up straighter, his mind whirling with the implications of that. She couldn't possibly be that inexperienced? Impossible.

He clenched his teeth and narrowed his eyes at her.

Keep focused. Women always lie about their experience.

He'd definitely found that one out the hard way.

She laughed without malice, the sound as musical as the classical *Bach* they had playing over the speakers. She glanced over his right shoulder, her eyes losing their focus as she remembered something in her past.

"It was clumsy, too short and..."

"And?"

She looked up at him then, her brown eyes shining with love. "Full of wonder and excitement. We'd been dating for over a year and he was moving away for work. We decided to have our first times together and it was...great. He was my best friend, and someone who really loved me."

Nate's belly tightened as he remembered the coldness of his first time. Some woman he'd met at a party who'd dragged him home and deflowered him without even removing her clothes, or his, for that matter. It had been one step better than masturbation.

He shuddered and clenched his teeth. He didn't like the feeling he was getting from this woman. Every one of his guards was slipping and his shoulders ached from trying to keep them up. She was faking it, she had to be. No one was this sweet.

"You can't be serious? Your partners since then must have known what they were doing."

Emily shrugged. "Yeah, I suppose, but I've never quite had that excitement again. The connection. I don't know..." Her voice trailed off again and she took another drink, her throat working as she swallowed hard. Were her eyes shimmering a little too?

Oh fuck, this girl can really turn it on.

"Sounds like you need a proper man, Emily."

Her eyes snapped up and he held her gaze, although part of him marveled at the smarmy tone he was using. He didn't want to bed her. A woman like this wouldn't survive one moment in his life and if she invoked the feelings he was most afraid of, then she'd make his life hell too.

She cocked her head to the side and blatantly ignored his statement.

"My turn. Last question. Hmmm..." She tapped her pointer finger to her chin and Nate picked up his knife and fork, cutting up his steak. He concentrated on that menial task and swallowed some of the juicy red meat while the strange woman in front of him thought of another probing question. Why was she interested in him anyway?

"Okay, if you could be anywhere in the world right now, where would it be and why?"

"That's easy. In my bed, naked with you."

She frowned at him and he grinned back, a tingle of happiness and power vibrating along his spine. Nothing like the honest truth to push someone to reveal their true self.

"That's not funny, Nate."

She put her fork to her lips and continued eating, her dark eyebrows drawn into a frown.

"I wasn't joking. I have a king size bed that is pure heaven, and I honestly couldn't think of anyone else I'd rather share it with at this point in time than you."

Again, she just frowned at him and he began to wonder when he'd lost his touch. Sure he was lying a bit—he didn't want to take her to bed—not yet, anyway. But what was with her resistance to him? These lines usually had women eating out of the palm of his hand.

"Anyway, your final question?" Her voice had taken a frosty tone that would have made an ice queen proud and Nathan found his chest and arm muscles tightening up in response to her change of attitude.

That's more like it sweetheart. Show me the real you.

"Why won't you sleep with me? There's obviously an attraction here."

"I don't sleep with people I work for, or with, Nathan. It's not smart."

Oh, I'm Nathan again, am I?

"So you agree we have an attraction?"

Her mouth thinned and she snorted out her nose. "You know there is, you're a very attractive man. But I'm not promiscuous and I respect myself a little bit more than resorting to being a notch on your bedpost."

Geez, she can't be serious.

"Hardly the worst thing that could happen, Emily."

Women in his past had given anything to be in his bed, literally trampling over their opposition to be the one on his mattress at the end of the night.

"Oh really, Nathan? Tell me more."

He let a smile spread across his lips and injected warmth into his tone as images flickered across his brain. Her on his bed, writhing with passion as she screamed his name and grabbed for the sheets with clenching hands.

"What could be better? A night full of passion between two consenting adults. It's true that I usually don't mix business with pleasure but I'm sure we're both mature enough not to let it get in the way of our work."

A voice inside his head was screaming at him to stop. He was talking to a woman who worked tirelessly for the underprivileged and classed her first time with her high school sweetheart as the best sex she'd ever had.

This woman had a *heart*. A quality that was so rare it called to his own long-dead organ and made him feel like a teenager again. An uncontrollable youngster. Not something he ever wanted to feel again.

She was hot, but she was definitely not a woman you could put into the one-night-stand category. And the main requirement of any woman he bedded was a lack of entanglement. They needed to be single, highly sexed and easily discarded. He didn't want to worry about hurting their feelings, or anything else for that matter.

Emily picked up her napkin and wiped her perfect mouth clean.

She stood up and smiled at him, the light in her cool, brown eyes now missing. "Thank you so much for dinner, Nathan. It was lovely. I will see you in a few days and I'll be in touch in regards to Eleanor's House."

Nathan pushed back his chair and jumped to his feet as Emily picked up her bag and began making her way to the front door. He took a few steps forward and grabbed her arm, halting her progress.

"Please let me go, Mr. Johnson."

The use of his title on her lips made his gut clench and he squeezed her arm as a cold panic shivered over his skin like a hive of bees.

"Hey, I thought we were having fun."

She pulled her arm out of his grasp with a sharp twist. "Good night, Mr. Johnson."

Emily walked out the door and he watched her go. That oversized suit swimming around her lush figure annoyed the hell out of him. He was sure she was quite beautiful under all of that black material. He'd seen it the night of the ball. Why didn't she have some decent clothes?

"Sir, have you finished your meal?" The maître d' stepped up next to him and Nathan forced himself to shake his head and walk back to his seat. There was no way he was letting a little thing such as this unsettle him.

He picked up his knife and fork and set about finishing his steak and the small pear and spinach salad. It was delicious, crisp and perfect for an evening meal.

It sat like lead in his gut. Heavy. Awkward. Painful.

His eyes darted to the double glass front doors and then back to the half-eaten risotto and the white napkin she'd tossed onto the table.

He pulled his phone out of his pocket and scrolled through several unread messages. His Uncle Nathan, the man he was named after, was first.

Bleh. No way. Next.

Two ex-lovers and a woman who had tried to pick him up at the airport.

He rolled his eyes and focused on the lewdness of one of the messages.

He waited for something to stir in his belly, a smile to crook his mouth or at least a tingle to say that he was interested.

Nothing.

Shit.

He called over the waiter, asked for the check and pulled out a credit card.

Thanks to Emily, his sex drive was gone and his interest in other, available women had diminished. When had he ever let a woman affect him in such a way? He searched his memory and came up with zip.

Double shit.

He actually liked Emily. He wanted to get to know her, talk to her again, and of course, get her into bed.

No bloody way.

It was too dangerous, for her and for him.

He growled in his throat as he pressed the dial button and attempted to get a cute blonde from a month ago on the phone. The ringtone sounded once and he hung up.

He shuddered in his seat for a moment and then forced a calm over himself.

He didn't need to prove anything to anyone. How many women had he bedded in his life? Too many to count. He didn't need another forced coupling with some random woman tonight. He'd go home and get an early night. He'd been burning the candle at both ends for a month. A whisky and some football were all he needed.

5

———————

$\mathcal{E}$mily sent the acceptance letter to Johnson Property Development the next day. She'd handled older men in powerful positions before and Nathan wasn't going to make her appear unprofessional.

She dove into her work, the hours flying by as one case after another took her attention. More money, more mergers, another day, another dollar.

A sigh settled in her chest and she let it escape. This was her life and she was grateful for it. Nothing to complain about.

"Good job with landing Nathan Johnson's company, Emily. I just heard."

Emily looked up and standing over her was her boss, Mr. Nelson. He was obviously on his way out for lunch, but he'd paused and was smiling at her through his large moustache.

She smiled up at the man she'd barely said two words to since she started two years ago. "Oh, thank you so much, Mr. Nelson."

The rotund, balding man gave her a once over, assessing look and strode towards the door.

"Wow. What did you do to land that deal? Sleep with the boss?"

Emily whirled around as Kristy spun her chair into Emily's cubicle.

"Hardly," Emily replied and glanced away before the truth of her misdemeanor became clear. She'd been accused of such a thing before in jest, but this was the closest it had come to being the truth.

"Then how'd you get a job there? I've heard they have a small internal team and rarely hire outside help."

A warm kernel of pride blossomed in Emily's belly but she tried to dismiss it as quickly as possible. Thinking too highly of Nate and his opinion of her was going to get her into trouble.

"It's probably just because I do so much volunteering at Eleanor's House. Nathan Johnson owns it." Which was technically the truth according to Kristy, although if Kristy was right and they never outsourced, she was indeed honored to be asked.

"Wow, maybe I should start volunteering there."

Emily laughed and shook her head. "Oh, I think that might be pushing it a bit, don't you, sweetie?"

Kristy stuck out her tongue and rolled out once again on her chair. Emily giggled again and got back to her own work with a smile still firmly placed on her lips. What an idea! Kristy volunteering at Eleanor's House! The girl was sweet, but her version of underprivileged contained people who didn't spend two hundred dollars on a pair of jeans. She wouldn't fit in at all.

An email dinged in her inbox and she opened it to find one from Martine.

Emily,

Thank you for your acceptance letter. It has been printed and filed, and if you could bring a printed and signed version of the official contract with you next time you're in the office, it would be much appreciated.

I have two new contracts for your perusal. Can you come in tomorrow?

Warm regards,

Martine.

Emily's eyebrows rose on her forehead as she stared at the email. Did they need her already? More hours meant more money. Well, okay then.

Hello Martine,

Yes, of course. I have a meeting in the morning but can give you the after-noon. 1 p.m. onwards.

Thanks

Emily.

Emily frowned at the email, one of the most casual business emails she had ever sent. Oh well, she was just copying the style of Nathan's assistant.

She pressed send and her belly clenched. Would that mean she'd have to see Nathan while she was there?

She shook her head and pulled out another file.

No. Concentrate on work. Nathan is nothing to you.

She put her head down and spent the rest of the day and night on her huge pile of paperwork that didn't give her much satisfaction, other than the billable hours she'd pull for the day. She'd have her house paid off in no time.

*J*AB, *jab, cross.*

Jab, jab, cross.

Nathan's hands ached but he kept up the pace, sweat dripping down his back as images of Emily's beautiful face floated around his mind.

"Argh!" He screamed and put all of his body weight into an uppercut and cross. The punching bag swung away and then came straight back at him.

He staggered away, his legs like jelly and his arms burning after almost an hour of body-punishing exercise.

He wasn't feeling like himself at all and it all came down to the woman he'd had dinner with last night.

Martine had informed him that Emily was coming in to deal with the contracts for the new commercial buildings he'd been commis-sioned for.

Great. Now he had to stay busy all day so that he didn't go

searching for her. Not that staying in his office should be hard. He had more work than he knew what to do with, but...

Fuck.

He pulled off the gloves, unwrapped his stinging hands from the clinging white tape and threw himself down into a chair.

He gazed around his home gym, fitted out with every modern machine and piece of exercise equipment. A deep exhaustion filled him up until he could barely lift his arms.

It was time for a hot shower and bed. Alone.

EMILY WALKED into Johnson Property Development with her head held high and an email on her phone from Cindy asking her if she'd managed to get Nathan to agree to speak at the anniversary night gathering.

And damn it, she hadn't. She'd had him all to herself two nights ago and she'd folded at the last minute. She'd shot out of there so bloody fast she hadn't thought about using the time with him for something more constructive.

Instead, she'd wanted to know about him and his past, his personality. She was intrigued and it was going to be the death of her, she was sure.

Stupid, stupid, stupid.

She took the lift up to the sixth floor and walked out into the foyer and turned into the office where Martine sat behind her pristine desk.

"Good afternoon, Martine."

"Emily. Lovely to see you. Please come this way. I've set up one of the conference rooms for you. I'm not sure how long you'll need but I work until nine most nights."

They stepped into a large, light-filled room and Emily placed her bag and briefcase down. This was so much better than her desk at her firm. She was going to enjoy working here.

"Thank you so much."

"Thank you. I'm glad you've come to work with us. You'll be an asset to the company, I'm sure."

Emily smiled as brightly as she could at the woman who had just managed to give her a truly warm and fuzzy feeling in her gut. She loved it when everyone in a business used the royal "we" or "us." It meant that the higher-ups had established a proper family and their employees felt it.

Which was a great reflection on Nathan.

She set to work and soon realized that she was going to be here all night.

As the sun set and darkness filled the room, Martine knocked and stepped into the conference room, which was currently set up as Emily's office.

"Still here, I see."

Emily glanced up, the orbits of her eyes throbbing with each pulse of her heart. She needed a break. "Yeah, I was hoping to get it all done tonight but I think I'll need to come back tomorrow."

Martine chuckled. "I expected you to take a week. I'm amazed if you're anywhere near finished."

Emily rubbed her tired eyes and stretched her arms above her head as she leaned back in her chair. "Well, thanks. I work fast when I'm not interrupted, which is great here."

"You want me to wait for you?"

Emily glanced back down at the folder she was holding and shook her head.

"No, I need to just tidy this up and then I'll head out. There's security around, yeah?"

"Of course, and there's a few others still working. So I'll see you tomorrow, Emily?"

"Absolutely."

The blonde assistant turned away and Emily called out to the woman who was the closest person to Nathan that she knew of. "Hey, Martine, can I ask you something?"

"Of course."

She bit her lip for a moment and weighed her words. She was going to need to say this right to get Martine on her side.

"I need to ask Mr. Johnson to make a speech at Eleanor's House and I was wondering how to approach him."

"Why are you asking me?"

Emily sat up straighter in her chair and leaned forward. "Because I know that you know him better than anyone. You've obviously worked together for a long time."

Emily let her lips lift in a soft smile as Martine's eyebrows lifted high.

Initially, she had assumed Martine was sleeping with Nathan, or at least held a candle for him. But something had changed since she'd spent some time with them and she now saw their relationship for what it was—a fantastic business relationship that was closer to the strength of a brother and sister. That was just her intuition speaking of course, though it was rarely wrong.

"We have. Almost ten years, actually."

Emily waited and Martine pursed her glossed lips for a moment.

"He won't want to talk at Eleanor's House. He doesn't enjoy speaking in public at all, and if he does, it's short and impersonal."

Emily rolled her eyes, remembering his speech from Saturday night. "Yeah, I've noticed."

She waited again, not wanting to push Martine to reveal confidences of a man she had worked with for a decade. Trust would be at a premium with a man like Nathan.

"You like him, don't you?"

The question surprised her and she gaped for a moment like a goldfish.

"Oh, ah…" Emily didn't know what to say. She looked away and took a few quick breaths, heat creeping into her cheeks.

Oh, crap.

She must've looked like a guilty schoolgirl caught in her crush on the school jock and it made her stomach churn.

Martine laughed softly. "I didn't mean to embarrass you. I just want to know if you have his best intentions at heart before I give you more information on him."

"Oh, of course, I do. I must admit that I do want him to talk for the sake of the women who benefit from his charity, but at the same time, I think he deserves to feel their actual gratitude. He seems very detached from it."

Martine nodded but didn't say anything else personal about Nate.

"All right. Well, all I can say is that his weekend is empty so he is available, and he's still in his office if you want to ask him."

She grinned at Emily and then left in a twirl.

The room was quiet except for the beat of her heart. It thumped against her ribs, her blood rippling along in her veins.

She took a deep, shuddering breath and pushed herself to her feet.

Martine knew what she was talking about and if she recommended talking to Nathan now, then Emily was going to do it.

She tugged on her jacket and lifted her head high. All she needed was ten minutes of his time.

And it was his own bloody charity!

With that thought firmly embedded in her mind, Emily strode out of her makeshift office, turned right and walked up to the large corner office that she knew to be Nathan's.

The lights were on and the door was wide open.

A gold name plaque was attached to the front door.

Nathan Johnson

CEO Johnson Property Development.

Her belly in knots despite her mental commands to her body to stop being crazy, she stepped into the doorway, lifted her hand and knocked on the wooden door. She could see him at his desk, staring down at some paperwork and her heart leapt as he lifted his head and stared at her. He had the most piercing blue eyes, and with his dark lashes and even darker hair, he sent her pulse into a fluttering overdrive.

"Emily."

"Hi, Nathan. Do you have a moment to talk?"

"Yes, of course, please come in."

He spoke in his business voice and despite her nervousness, she walked into the room and took a seat opposite him. There was something fraudulent about that voice that she didn't like, but it was better than the smarmy one he'd used to try to coax her into his bed.

"What can I help you with, Emily?"

"I was hoping I could speak to you about Saturday night. My supervisor emailed me again today asking if it was possible that you come and speak at Eleanor's Charity for the ten-year anniversary. We would only need you for about ten minutes—"

"I'm afraid I'm busy on Saturday night."

Emily shut her mouth, which was still open since she was only halfway through finishing her sentence.

She bit her lip and stared at him for a moment, weighing up her options of fighting for what she wanted versus conceding defeat and leaving. Giving up was never really an option for her and there was some devil inside of her that really wanted to see what Nate was made of.

"Ah, I checked with Martine and she said you were available."

Nathan glanced away, clenching his jaw as his face contorted with anger.

When he finally looked back at her his blue eyes were hard.

Oops, maybe that wasn't the best way to start.

"Well, Martine doesn't know everything I do with my calendar and my life. I have made plans and you don't need to know what they are."

Emily took a deep breath and lay her hands gently in her lap. Patience was the key with this one.

"Nate." She let his nickname hang in the air, hoping it would soften him a little. "Would it be possible to give us ten minutes of your time? We can be totally flexible. First thing at 6 p.m. or even midnight. Whatever works for you, I will make sure there are people there to hear your speech."

Nathan relaxed back into his chair and stared at her through slitted eyelids.

"How much is it worth to you, Emily?"

And the smarmy tone was back.

Emily's spine tightened and pulled her up until she was certain she could balance a book on her head. "I don't know what you mean."

"Come on, Emily...Emmy...what do you prefer?"

"No one's ever called me Emmy."

It sounded strange and she wasn't sure it suited her at all.

"Good...now, Emmy, how far would you go to guarantee my attendance Saturday night?"

She forced a soft laugh through her lips. Surely he was joking?

"I'm not going to sleep with you, if that's what you're asking."

His silken chuckle made her gasp, heat pooling between her thighs at that delicious sound. He was one silver-tongued man.

"I would never expect a woman to sleep with me just to get something from me. God forbid." His tone dripped sarcasm and her chest tightened at the well-aimed arrow.

"Touché, Mr. Johnson."

Her gaze dropped to the floor and she struggled to think of what to say next. So many other women would have jumped into his bed in the hopes of money, prestige or at least flashy holidays and gifts. Although she would never sleep with him, his comment made her feel cheap for even attempting a bad flirtation.

"I was being ironic, Emily."

She lifted her head when his tone returned to normal. "But I don't have anything to offer you other than my heartfelt thanks. You own the place so you know there's no money to pay you. You have built such an amazing charity, Nate. You really should be there to see it celebrate such an achievement. So many people want to thank you for everything you've done for them, and you deserve the praise. You really do."

Nathan's eyes opened wide, his armor of disdain falling away like a visible skin.

"Have dinner with me again."

"What?" Couldn't he be serious?

"I want to get to know you better."

She shook her head, twisting her hands in her lap. "I'm not sure that's a good idea."

"If you have dinner with me tomorrow night, I'll drop in at your party Saturday night."

Oh, he was canny. Offering her the one thing she wanted. "No matter what?"

"No matter what, but I'm not speaking."

We'll see about that.

She tilted her head to the side and offered him a soft smile. "You're sure I can't tempt you into it?"

"You could tempt the devil himself to give up Hell—but I'll hold back. Thanks."

Wow.

She blinked and mulled over his words once again.

"I think that's the best compliment I've ever received."

He broke eye contact and dropped his head, shuffling papers around on his desk. "Yeah, well, don't get used to it. I'm not known for my compliments."

Her mouth twisted as a giggle bubbled up inside her. No, he was known for his charm, his money, his work ethic and his untouchable shield of indifference.

"Don't worry, Nate. I won't tell anyone."

She stood up and backed towards the door. "I'll see you tomorrow night, then?"

"Yes."

She turned and fled, the air in her lungs evaporating as the giggle burst free.

He was coming to the party!

She packed up her laptop and put the files away into a cabinet inside the next room. She'd be back here tomorrow for work and dinner, and the women at the shelter would finally get to meet the man who made it all possible.

Nate ran a hand through his hair and powered off his computer. He couldn't do any more tonight. His brain was fried, and now that he'd smelled Emily's beautiful fruity scent, his mind was filled with her smiling face.

Not great when you were trying to design a forty floor skyscraper.

He pulled on his jacket, loosened his tie and undid the top button on his shirt with a groan. As he moved towards the door, his back ached across his shoulder blades and he stretched his back until he heard the joints give a pop.

"Argh. Better."

He strolled towards the elevator and saw Emily look behind her as the doors dinged open and she hurried inside.

A grin tugged up his lips as he increased the speed of his stride to step into the lift just as the doors slid shut.

He heard her sharp intake of breath and his heart began to thump in his chest. Why had he done that?

The air in the lift was hot and he was far too aware of her body next to his, smaller, softer and ready for the taking.

"Nate."

His control snapped and he whirled her towards the wall, their briefcases clattering to the floor. He pressed her into the shining stainless steel and stared down into her wide brown eyes, her pink lips parted in invitation.

He didn't stop to ask her, he just let his lips drop and took her mouth in a kiss. She moaned and pressed into him, sliding her hands up his arms and into his hair.

Oh fuck, she tastes so good.

A groan rumbled in his chest as he opened her lips and let his tongue delve into her sweetness, the fruitiness of her taste as intoxicating as any expensive wine.

He ran his hands around her waist and pulled her as close as possible, her pelvis cradling his cock, which was rapidly filling with blood and throbbing in his pants.

The doors dinged open and Emily froze in his arms. He pulled himself away from her heat and cold swept in between them.

She was an erotic vision for his passion-hazed eyes. Her hair was slightly mussed, her mouth swollen. He could barely control the urge to press the top floor button and take her back to his office.

Emily's brown eyes were wide and drugged, her once-pink lips now a deep red and parted as she took shallow breaths.

"Sir, do you need an escort to your car?"

The security guard's voice broke through the hot stare between them and Emily wrapped her arms around her body.

"Ah, I don't, but Emily may. Is your car far?"

She pushed off the wall and picked up her briefcase that lay belly down on the floor. She stepped out of the elevator and Nate walked out behind her, the older man in uniform looking between them and then pulling on his mask of indifference.

At least she has all of her clothes on.

"My car is about two blocks away."

The security guard nodded and put his hands on his hips. He'd be older than her father but at least he afforded Emily some safety on her dark walk.

Nate would love to offer to walk her out but he wasn't sure she'd be totally safe with him. Adrenaline was still pumping through his body, his arms and back bunched with muscled strength as the caveman in him demanded he get her back and finish what they started.

"Thanks, Sam."

The security guard nodded and Emily cast a glance back at him before she exited the building through the double glass doors.

Nate headed out the small door next to the security guard station and stepped up to his luxury sports car.

He had all of the things he'd set out to achieve by thirty-five and he should be happy. His company made more money than he could spend and his mother's charity was thriving. He got into his car and drove home to his high-rise apartment, alone and not feeling as happy about it as he had, just last week.

6

_____

$\mathcal{E}$mily's leg shook so much her desk rattled. It was ten to two and she needed to head over to Johnson Property Development, but she had no idea what would happen when she got there.

An email pinged in her inbox.

Hi Emily,

Just confirming you'll be coming in this afternoon?

I need to arrange conference rooms.

Thanks

Martine.

A groan left her lips and she slumped onto her desk, her forehead hitting the wood in a dramatic approach to the situation.

"Hey, what's up with you?" Kristy pulled her chair up next to Emily's and tapped her nails on Emily's desk.

Emily groaned again and pulled herself up to stare at her friend.

"I have to head over to Johnson Property Development and I can't be bothered. I have too much other work to do." Well, that was efficient lying, she had to admit. She wasn't usually quite so fast.

"You're kidding me? Since when do you pass up the opportunity for more work?"

She was right, the answer was never. More billable hours, more money for her company and more bonuses for her. That was what she was here for. Money. Security. Her house.

With that in mind, she straightened up and took a few calming breaths.

"You're right, Kristy. I better get going, then."

She grabbed her phone and her briefcase and smiled at one of the few friends she had at work. She didn't give Kristy enough credit and she should. Sure, the girl had grown up with a silver spoon in her mouth, but she'd been nothing but nice to Emily since day one.

Ten minutes later, she arrived at Johnson Property Development, took the lift up to the sixth floor, greeted Martine and slipped straight into the conference room she'd used the night before. Her heart was banging against her ribs and her senses were on high alert as she scurried around. She set up on the opposite side of the table this time so that she could see everyone who approached. Unfortunately that meant that she had her back to the city view and she jumped every time someone walked past.

He'd kissed her. Nathan Johnson had kissed her in an elevator last night. She had to deal with that fact, and more to the point, that she'd liked it. More than *liked* it. It had rocked her world and she'd spent most of last night in bed reliving the moments his hard body had been pressed against hers and his mouth had been transforming her life.

That was how a kiss was meant to be. Heated looks, wobbly knees and lips that made every thought fly out of your head.

Not that she'd experienced it before. But she'd read books. And it was textbook perfect. Romance to a tee.

She pulled out her files and started arranging her work across the conference room table. She had to get through these contracts and then she had to prepare for their dinner.

She blew out a breath as her heart sank.

That was the real reason her heart was racing and she couldn't concentrate properly. She had committed to tonight's dinner and she had to go through with it.

But how to do that when his interest in her was more than professional? Normally she would fall back on her natural distrust of men.

But nothing about him tweaked those instincts. She wanted to help him, see what was behind all the bullshit he presented to the world.

The other problem was personal, and she knew it. She was attracted to him, very attracted to him. Her very skin was holding its breath for the moment he would touch her again.

Could she break through that armor to see what sort of man lay beneath? It was definitely a challenge she could rise to, but it was a dangerous move. Professionally and personally. Nathan Johnson was a major league heartbreaker and she wasn't sure she would survive him. She was already more invested in this relationship than she'd ever been with anyone. He was her boss at her paid job, technically her boss at the charity she loved and had given her the best kiss of her life.

She blew out a long breath, shook her head and put her glasses on her nose. Time to concentrate. Dinner would come soon enough.

And it did. Just as she was finishing up on the file in front of her there was a knock on the door. She dragged her tired eyes up from the screen of her laptop and saw Nathan standing in the doorway, leaning against the architrave. Heat flushed into her cheeks and she yanked off her glasses.

"You ready to go?"

She tidied up the papers in front of her and heaved a sigh. "Yeah, I suppose so. What time is it?" She glanced at the clock to see 7 p.m. "Geez, where does the time go? Yeah, give me five to just pack up?"

Nathan nodded and walked away and her breath shuddered in her throat. Her pulse had picked up and her stomach now ached in a way that wasn't about hunger.

She packed up and dug her fingernails into her palms as she stared out the window and took a few deep breaths.

She'd emailed Cindy to let her know that Nathan would be at the cocktail party, and she was absolutely ecstatic about it. Emily had said that she'd work on him about the speech.

With one final, calming breath, she turned and picked up her briefcase. Time to face the music.

She walked through the door and saw the dark suit by the elevator.

Her heart fluttered in her chest.

Many men cut an impressive shape in a suit, but Nathan looked monumentally breathtaking. His wide shoulders spoke of strength and masculinity, his thin waist told of his youth and fitness.

"Where are we going tonight?"

She strolled up beside him and smiled, the haunted look in his eyes causing a sudden lurch to her belly.

"Are you all right, Nate?"

NATHAN'S BREATH came in short pants as he struggled to get his heart to slow down.

Her voice, so light and happy, had him projecting into a future of late dinners, laughter, and contentment. He'd never known such a thing before with a woman. Some distant memory of his early childhood often plagued him. He'd known happiness once, and the sound of laughter. It had been a very long time since those moments, though.

She was still looking at him expectantly and he cleared his throat while he searched for the last thing she'd said.

"Yeah, I'm fine. I hadn't really thought about it. Do you have a preference?"

He ran a shaking hand through his hair and tugged at his already loosened tie. He unraveled it and tucked it into his pocket. Happiness literally shone off Emily like a ring around the moon.

How did she do that and why hadn't he seen it in anyone else before?

"There's a burger place around the corner that's really good."

He stared at her and concentrated on keeping his jaw firmly shut. If he'd been a cartoon he could see his mouth dropping open and his tongue rolling out onto the ground.

She was a woman who was being taken out for dinner by a man who would pay for just about anything she wanted, and she requested burgers?

To use his grandmother's old one-liner, *blow me down with a feather.*

"Sure."

What else could he say? He hadn't eaten a burger in more years than he cared to remember.

The elevator dinged open and Emily stepped inside, hugging her briefcase to her chest with a wobbly smile.

He chuckled and stepped in beside her, letting his shoulders drop down as his body began to relax into her company.

"Nervous, Emily?"

She squeaked and jumped away from him a little.

A chuckle rumbled out of his throat as he rocked back on his heels. He wasn't going to jump her again in the lift, the mood wasn't right for one thing and the last thing he wanted to do was give her more ammunition to fire at him. He was going to need his wits about him as it was.

"I don't want to cross any more lines."

He laughed aloud at that one.

"Really? Well, keep those hot lips on that side of the lift and we'll be fine."

"Oh!" The indignant noise and the sound of the briefcase dropping onto the floor made him smirk, but he didn't glance her way until the doors dinged open once again.

"Lead on, Emmy."

She lifted her nose in the air and stomped out of the lift.

His lips kept on smirking as he followed the princess through the glass doors and onto the street.

"It's this way." She nodded to the right and they walked side by side along the sidewalk, the city now out of peak time had a nice hum to it without the busy traffic noises.

They turned right, left, then moved up a small alley Nathan had never seen before.

Emily stopped suddenly and then pushed open a wooden door with no sign on it.

"After you." Nathan held out his hand and she bobbed a short curtsy before giving him a smile and heading into the restaurant.

A sense of relief swam through him and he frowned, searching through his feelings for why that one had surfaced. He stepped into the brightly lit restaurant and followed Emily to a small booth when he realized that he'd been worried that she'd take his joke in the elevator seriously.

Wow. Since when do you care so much about how a woman feels?

"Can I get you something to drink first?" The bubbly waitress hurried up, took their drink orders and bustled away again.

"It's busy." And cheap.

Emily looked around with a smile. "Yeah, it's always buzzing. I've come here a few times and I've never seen it empty."

"You already know what you're having, I suppose." He pointed to her closed menu and she gave him a sunshine-type smile.

"Yep."

He glanced down the menu and when the little hippie waitress spun by again he ignored his normally strict protein intake and ordered the biggest burger and fries combo he could find. With Emily he was eighteen again, so he may as well eat like it too.

"You'll love that. I shared it with a friend last time we were here. If you don't eat it all, you can take it home."

The hairs on the back of his neck prickled and he straightened his spine. Sharnie, his girlfriend in University use to sound like that. When she was being nice, she giggled and spoke with that happiness vibrating from Emily.

The next scene flashed into his mind. The screaming, the pain in his hands, his face. Never wanting to be his father. Never…

"What's with the good girl act, Emily? I have to ask you. Seriously. Does everyone buy into this routine?"

"What?" Her tone was confused, and a little wounded.

He turned his eyes away, his neck aching from the strain he was putting on the muscles.

"Look…I think I'll go."

"No."

Nathan's hand whipped out and grabbed her thigh, holding her to the seat. "You want me to come to your stupid party on Saturday night? You'll stay and have dinner with me."

Her fingers grabbed hold of his hand and pried his grip from her thigh. He could have held on of course, but he let her go because he was doing the wrong thing.

"Mr. Johnson. You are insulting me and confusing me. I suggest you work out what the hell you want and get back to me."

She swung around and jumped off the stool, walking straight for the door of the restaurant.

"Fuck."

He closed his eyes for a moment, his hands shaking as they lay on his thighs. What the hell was wrong with him? He tossed some cash on the counter.

"Emily. Wait!"

He headed out after her, reaching her as she hit the main road. "Stop. Please."

She whirled on him, her mouth grim and her eyes fiery. "What the fuck is wrong with you? Seriously! I have tried to be nice. I've tried to be professional. I've tried not to let my natural distrust of men make me hate you because I think what you've achieved and who you are, are pretty bloody amazing. So why?"

She screamed and began charging down the street again.

He took off after her, a weird smile tugging up his lips as his belly twisted with a strange laugh. She was an odd creature. Honest, brave, a little naïve and beautiful in her wildness.

His hand reached out for her arm once again. "Emmy, please wait."

She whirled to face him and he swallowed a groan at the spectacular picture she made before him. Her cheeks were slashed with color and her eyes were bright.

"You have to be the most unique woman I have ever come across."

She growled a little in anger between her clenched jaw and he bit the bullet to grovel. "I'm sorry. That was uncalled for. And stupid."

"Why don't you believe I am who I am? I've never lied to you. Not once! Even when I had to tell you about my stupid father."

She broke off with a weird choking sound and a strange tightness spread across his chest. "I meant what I said. I am sorry. Sometimes you remind me of someone I once knew, and it brings out some old, bad memories. It wasn't your fault."

He reached up a hand and cupped her face, unable to stop himself from touching her.

She glared at him but didn't move away, huffing at him. "You know I should hate you for turning on me all the time. I never know if I'm dealing with Dr. Jekyll or Mr. Hyde. Nate, Nathan or Mr. Johnson. It's not fair."

Something happened at that moment he hadn't experienced in sixteen years. The unbelievably strong urge to say *I love you* to a woman. The words flowed through his subconscious and to his lips and he grabbed her and pulled her close to stop them from exploding out.

She moaned against him as he crushed her body to his, prying her lips open with his own to taste her sweetness again.

He kissed her gently once more and then pulled away, not wanting to add too much to his list of transgressions.

She stared at him, her pink lips shining in the evening light and her eyes wide.

"I don't get you at all."

He smiled, shrugged and thrust both hands in his pockets. "You don't need to."

"I don't want to go out for dinner anymore, Nate. I'm exhausted."

Her shoulders drooped.

"It's fine. I'll walk you to your car."

"Okay, thanks."

They turned right and began to walk, a strolling pace that suited him well. They could talk a little.

EMILY REACHED up and grabbed the elastic band wrapped around her bun, tugging and pulling at it until she undid both the bun and the ponytail, the pain across her skull easing as she shook out her hair.

"Ah, that feels better."

"You look beautiful with your hair down."

Emily rolled her eyes and slid a sidelong glance at the man walking beside her. She wasn't touching that one. She knew she wasn't beautiful, but she didn't want to get into an argument with him about it, so she focused on what she actually wanted to know.

"We have about five minutes until we reach my car, so it's my turn to talk." She bit her lip. There was nothing to lose now. She'd practically spelled it out to him how much she liked him. "No, I'll beg. Please do a speech for us on Saturday night? Ten minutes, that's all we need."

He blew out a breath and started kicking the sidewalk like a four-year-old ruining his shoes. "And what do you want me to say?"

Whoa, he's thinking about it! Stay calm.

"Tell people why you started Eleanor's House and they'll be happy. You're the only reason that so many women are independent and are able to live their own lives now."

And I think they should know who you are so they can thank you.

"I don't like questions. I don't want the thanks."

Damn.

His voice was far too icy. She'd never get anywhere with him in this state of mind.

"Fine, just come and I'll do a speech thanking you. How's that?"

He stopped in the street and she whirled to face him, raising her eyebrows in silent question.

"You'll stand up in front of everyone and thank me for building Eleanor's House?"

"Yes, of course."

His headshake was almost violent. "No, thank you. I'll come, but I don't want any acknowledgment."

"I can't do that. It's all about Eleanor's House and you are such a big part of that."

His jaw clenched. He looked away towards the building with his name on it.

"Keep it professional, Emily."

She waited for him to look back at her and risked a small smile at him. "But you said Eleanor's House was personal."

He practically growled at her like a bear with a sore paw, the sexy rumble coming from his chest.

"I know I did... but…oh, for fuck's sake, Emily."

He glared at her, both hands on his hips as he did his obvious best to appear scary.

"Okay, okay, nothing too personal. Got it."

They'd reached her car so she gave him a smile and got inside, watching him as he walked back to his car at the company carpark. She'd sidestepped the issue so that he'd think she'd given up, but inside her brain she was plotting for Saturday night. She was convinced that if she got Nathan to accept the praise he was due, she'd be able to get past all the bluster and coldness. There had to be a real man beneath the façade. Surely?

7

———————

*E*mily spent all day on Saturday at Eleanor's House, setting up tables, cleaning windows and blowing up balloons. They had next to no money to decorate but they'd all put in and had given a real party flavor to the large common room that served as a lounge room for the women who lived at Eleanor's House.

"I can't believe you've got the owner coming to the party!" Tiffany, a young woman who only recently came to stay at the charity house, bounced around the room.

Emily laughed and grinned at the girl who brought joy with her wherever she went. She, like all the others, did not deserve what fate had served up.

"He's more the founder than the owner. But yeah, Nathan Johnson's coming tonight."

Tiffany danced out of the room and Cindy stared at her with wide eyes. "I can't believe he's coming either. I've worked here for six years and I've barely seen him."

"Wow, really?" Emily asked as she set up cups and plates.

"What's he like?"

Oh, how to even begin to describe Nate.

"Ah... hmm... he's arrogant, smart, two-faced and ..."

Cindy chuckled and handed her another lot of cups. "Sounds charming."

"Oh, he's that too." She winked at Cindy and her friend laughed.

"You sound as though you like him."

Oh, I do. But only one or two of his personalities. Not all of them, and that's the problem. "He's hard to hate."

"Why would you want to hate him?"

"I mean… I always try to maintain a professional distance." Now she was embarrassing herself. *Stop talking!* Her face was burning up.

"Uh-oh, you *really* like him!"

Oh, God. Leave me alone.

"Oh, shush."

Emily finished party preparations, rushed home and got ready, her excitement pumping through her so fast she could barely feel her feet touching the ground. She turned once in the mirror to make sure she hadn't inherited wings, but she has relieved to see they were obviously still invisible.

If everything went to plan, she'd be giving someone a special gift tonight.

Nathan swallowed hard, the awkwardness of the lump in his throat paling in comparison to the amount of tightness in his chest. He'd never been inside Eleanor's House.

Ever.

He'd drawn the designs for the building, spent a year raising the money and fighting the council, but in eleven years since the conception of the project, he'd never walked through the front doors.

He took one shuddering breath after another, his gaze magnetically drawn to his mother's name, which hung above the large steel-enforced doors.

He'd wanted a safe haven for these women and that had meant top security from the outset.

A large man stood at the door with a clipboard.

He stepped up, clearing his throat. "Nathan Johnson."

The burly security guard nodded once and opened the door for him.

One more quick breath and he stepped inside, the atmosphere of heat, too many people, and happy music hitting him with the strength of a boxer's glove to the gut.

Wow. His eyes roamed up and down the walls. He was glad to see that the architrave was as detailed as he had once drawn. So much of it was how he had designed it, but the entrance was bigger than he had imagined. They'd strung up some cheap streamers and taped up some balloons too. He stood in a central welcoming reception area with many doors that lead to two main hallways, and if he remembered correctly, there should be a large lounge at the back of the reception. *That's probably where they're holding the party.*

The doors behind the reception burst open and Emily emerged, laughter and modern radio music accompanying her like a cloud of happiness.

"Nathan!" She hurried forward with a huge smile on her face, her simple black and white halter-neck dress accentuating her spectacular figure.

The tightness in his chest returned with the squeeze of a boa constrictor.

"I'm so glad you came. I was worried you wouldn't. Come on in."

You have no idea how close I came to not showing up here tonight. Or ever...

She tucked her hand into his elbow and gently ushered him forward. He let her lead him—didn't seem much point in fighting her.

They stepped through the doors and the scene before him made his heart rate race. Women everywhere. And children. Everywhere.

More brightly colored balloons and streamers adorned the walls, and tables of drinks and food lined the walls. It looked like a kid's birthday party. One he'd never had but had always longed for.

"I know it's not ritzy or anything, but..."

"It's great, Emily. You guys have done an amazing job."

She gave him another brilliant smile, squeezed his arm and then ran off to talk to some other women, leaving him alone in a sea of uncomfortable happiness.

He didn't know what he was doing and for the first time in a very long time, he didn't have Martine to co-ordinate him or a speech to cling to.

His throat tightened, his palms sweated.

"Hi, I'm Cindy. You must be Mr. Johnson."

Nathan turned towards the older blonde who had approached him, her kind face ringing a bell in his head.

"You can call me Nathan, Cindy. You're the coordinator of Eleanor's House."

She inclined her head gracefully. "I am, and it's been an honor to work for your foundation, Nathan."

He smiled back but had nothing else to say. It had been a long time since he'd had a hand in the hiring of the staff here. He couldn't remember a thing about the woman in front of him, except that she did a great job of running everything.

Women jostled around him and he felt the snake around his chest squeeze tighter. He'd set this charity up ten years ago, raised money to run it and accepted people's accolades for his philanthropic approach to life. But those thanks had been from women with too much money, or those wanting to jump into his bed.

Not those that were actually in his mother's situation and required help.

He took another deep breath.

"Are you all right, Nathan?"

He nodded but Cindy continued to peer at him with a knowing look, then dragged him towards the drinks table, pouring him a glass of water and pressing it into his hands. "Please drink, you look like you need it."

Nathan downed the water in two gulps, releasing a breath as the cool liquid slid down into his belly. "I'm all right. Thank you."

"You don't enjoy crowds?"

A chuckle escaped him as he stared at the woman in front of him. How had no one else ever picked up on that except her? He made a mental note to increase her salary. This woman deserved praise and a raise. She was obviously very good at her job.

"No, I don't."

"Well, we'll start the speeches soon, and you'll be able to leave straight after if you want. I'm sorry I didn't realize that you weren't comfortable in these sorts of settings, or I would never have pushed Emily into getting you here tonight."

So another thing to thank Cindy for. He hadn't given a thought to the driving force behind why he and Emily had been spending so much time together, and why she'd allowed herself to be talked into so many dinners.

"It's fine. Ten years is quite an achievement for any association, and I should be here to celebrate tonight."

"Yes, you should. This house has saved countless lives, mine included."

"Pardon me?"

He didn't remember her as being someone who stayed at Eleanor's House as a client. It hadn't been on her resume. He would have made a note of that.

"Oh, not as literally as some of the women, but when I applied for this position I was almost bankrupt and my husband had left me and my daughter with nothing. If you, or whomever hired me, hadn't given me this chance then I don't know where I would be."

Oh.

Cindy looked up at him then with such a warm expression, he felt some of the ice around his heart crack and shatter. There was no calculation in her eyes, no aloof posture, only pure heart and thanks pouring from her. He hadn't known women like this existed.

"I… ah…" His throat tightened and he glanced away. What did you say to someone like that?

"Nathan, Nathan!" He turned towards Emily's voice and her radiance shone straight at him as she rushed forward, her hands flapping.

"We're about to do the speeches, are you sure you don't want to speak?"

"Very sure."

A fleeting flash of disappointment crossed over her face and then she took Cindy's hand and they both walked over to the makeshift stage and podium. He stood back and stepped up close to the refreshment tables, his back as close to the wall as he could get it.

The speeches began and Cindy thanked everyone for coming, listed off some rather impressive statistics on how many people they'd helped over the years and the coming improvements and expansion.

Nathan let his brain drift in and out. The atmosphere of the room, although weirdly different and crowded, which would generally put him in a shitty mood, had him relaxing. His shoulders were dropped, his belly had calmed and his chest was no longer restricting his breathing.

There was a family feel to the room that he'd felt only at rare friends' homes in primary school. Photos everywhere, too much food. That strange warmth and clutter to a home where you know only good things happen.

A round of applause signaled the end of Cindy's speech and Emily stood, her full cheeks pink as she nervously glanced around the room and found him. Her smile brightened and she cleared her throat, speaking into the microphone.

"I feel so honored to be standing here today, in what I consider one of the best not-for-profit organizations in Australia." A round of applause greeted that heartfelt proclamation and Nathan grinned at the woman glowing from the center of the room. She was definitely one of a kind.

Tonight he could see in her that beautiful young woman he met in the foyer of a grand hotel only last weekend. Glowing with happiness and good health, her aura had attracted him like no other had ever done.

"I recently had the pleasure of meeting the man who set up the foundation that built Eleanor's House, at a fundraiser where he was putting plans together for the extensions that Cindy talked about tonight. No one would recognize him because he never puts himself out into society proclaiming to be the hero I know he is, but I want to take the opportunity to publically thank Nathan Johnson, the man standing at the back of the room in the black suit with his arms crossed." Fifty sets of eyes turned on him and Nathan's stomach literally flipped over inside his belly.

Cold prickled his skin and his cheeks drained of all blood. He tightened the arms that already wrapped around his chest and squeezed.

So much for enjoying the atmosphere.

EMILY WATCHED the horror-struck look as the color drained from Nathan's cheeks and she felt a moment's regret as acid dropped into the pit of her stomach.

He needed to know what he'd done. His ability to hold himself aloof from everyone needed to be rectified. He'd constructed an ice tower around himself, it was obvious. But it was killing him.

She pushed forward. "Nathan deserves to know how much he has affected everyone's lives, so without rushing him, please feel free to speak to him throughout the night. He is a humble man, and I think it's important he knows what his hard work has achieved. Thank you and enjoy the night."

There was silence and then a round of applause as people started to surge towards Nathan. Women, young and old, some dragging children, others by themselves. But all of them were walking towards Nate, one of the only men in the room.

Emily glanced towards him and saw him backing towards the door. No, he couldn't be leaving.

She rushed forward, cutting through the throng of women who all wanted to tell their stories to Nathan.

His blue eyes were icy as she drew up next to him and turned to stand in front of him, blocking him like a shield with her body. She held up both of her hands and spoke to the nearest people.

"Remember what I said about Nathan always working in the shadows. Please give him a little space until he settles in. Go enjoy the food and we'll mingle in a moment."

The women all nodded and grinned at her with huge smiles, turning away with lingering glances at their handsome savior.

"I cannot believe you did that to me."

The malice in his voice made her cringe as she turned around slowly and looked up at him. "What are you talking about? I thought you'd like hearing from the women you've helped so much."

"Me? I didn't even want to come to this and now you're pushing me straight into the limelight when you know I hate it."

Emily took a step back, taking a hard look at the man in front of her before swallowing hard. He was upset. His cheeks were slashed with an angry red, his jaw was tight and his arms were crossed across his chest.

Maybe I pushed this a little too hard.

"I'm sorry, I didn't mean to do that. I thought you'd be okay with it."

He made a growling sound and pushed past her, his tall figure cutting through the crowd like a hot knife through butter.

She watched him go with a knot in her gut. Damn. How had she mucked that up so badly?

Cindy came rushing up to her. "What happened? Did he leave?"

"Yeah, ah… he was angry I told everyone to come and talk to him."

Cindy grimaced. "Yeah, I thought that was a bit much, considering how private he is."

"What do you mean? I thought it would be good for him."

Cindy sighed. "His body language was obviously uncomfortable. He doesn't like crowds and he's never stepped into Eleanor's House for a reason, Em. It's not really your place to throw him straight into the deep end."

Cindy's words hit home hard and Emily glanced away, her eyes stinging with unshed tears. The words of disappointment from a woman she admired so much made her want to cry. She worked so hard to do the right thing, and her she'd hurt someone she cared about. How had she not picked up on that?

"I didn't mean to upset him."

Cindy lay a hand on Emily's arm and Emily raised her wet eyes to look at her friend and mentor. "I know."

Cindy gave Emily a small smile and walked away, leaving Emily alone with her stomach ache.

BY THE END of the night, Emily was ready to do anything to make it up to Nathan. The more she thought about it, the more she hated herself for pushing him into such an uncomfortable position. He may be an internationally successful businessman and a major hard-ass as far as most people were concerned, but if anyone knew that he had a soft side, it was her.

And she felt like she'd taken advantage of it. Of him.

Shit! I pushed him too far, and now anything might happen.

Strangely, she wasn't afraid of how he'd punish her. He could get her fired from her corporate position, kick her out of Eleanor's House and personally humiliate her. But she wasn't concerned about that. She was worried about him. Worried sick.

And that was the strangest thing about all this. Since when did she care more about a man whom she barely knew than her livelihood?

She smiled and chatted through the evening, even getting onto the dance floor with some of the older children when the music got cranked up, but inside she was battling the spreading cold and sadness.

Midnight arrived and the music was turned off, the food and drinks were cleared away and the lights went down.

Emily snuck into the office and pulled out the files on the new extension. She was sure she could find Nathan's address in there somewhere. She had to apologize.

And she couldn't wait until Monday.

She dug through a pile of paperwork, scanning and flicking through. Finally, she found the piece of paper she was looking for. She made note of the address in her phone and put everything away in its place.

Surely he wouldn't throw her out if she came to apologize?

Call him maybe? Or message him, but she wanted to make sure he knew how sorry she was, and there was only one way to do that.

She said goodbye to everyone and kissed Cindy goodnight. Meanwhile, her heart was thundering in her chest as she clung to her mobile phone.

When she got into her car she plugged in his address, unsurprised to find he lived only a few streets from his work. Five minutes, max.

She drove there carefully, her hands shaking as she weighed the wisdom of her midnight apology idea. She pulled up outside a tall apartment building, her belly in knots and her mouth suddenly dry as a desert.

Licking her lips, she swallowed hard. It was twelve-thirty. Would he be asleep already? It was a Saturday night so she hoped not.

She stepped out of her car and stepped up to the intercom barring her way into the expensive building.

She bit her lip. What to do now?

She glanced down at her phone. Apartment thirty-two, which may be on level three, or it may be way up the top. Hmmm.

A couple walked around the corner, arm in arm and opened the door with an electronic key.

Brilliant!

Emily smiled at them and followed them inside, trying to appear like she fit in by not looking around too much. It was a beautiful building, though. Modern, almost too clean.

She stuck close by as the couple walked into the lift and used their key once again to gain admittance to the other floors.

She tried not to stare at the attractive, obviously moneyed older couple. She hadn't even thought about how she was going to get into his apartment.

"You look lost, do you need some help?" the woman in the elevator asked her and Emily jumped a little, blood rushing into her cheeks as she met the blonde lady's eye.

"Ah, yes. I wanted to come visit a friend, as a surprise, and I know they live in apartment thirty-two, but I'm not sure what level that's on."

The lady smiled brightly and pointed to level three and pushed the button so that it lit up yellow.

"Level three, apartment two."

"Thank you so much."

The doors dinged open a moment later on level three and she jumped off, her heart thumping in her chest as she followed the sign to apartment two. She'd expected something a bit more *penthouse*, flashy and super-expensive. But she was also a little relieved that Nathan wasn't pretentious.

What a ridiculous thought. He's your boss, nothing else.

She raised her hand to knock and then stopped. It was almost 12:45 a.m. now, what was she doing?

Ah, shit. You're an idiot.

She closed her eyes and hung her head, taking in slow breaths through her nose. She'd come this far, what the hell was she going to do now?

Opening her eyes, she glanced behind her at the wall. Perhaps she should sit down and wait until morning?

She snorted at herself and then squared her shoulders.

A plan formed in her head. She'd knock twice, softly. If he was up he'd hear her, if he was asleep she would leave and no one would be any wiser.

Clenching her jaw so that her teeth pressed together, she made a fist with her hand and knocked gently on the door below the silver numbers three and two.

She waited. Nothing.

A shuddering breath wracked her body, her belly flipping inside her like a landed fish. One more time.

She knocked a little louder, held her breath, then let it out.

Nothing.

Relief came out in a deep sigh but a niggling amount of disappointment surprised her as it crept up the back of her spine. Had she really wanted to see him that much?

She turned on the ball of her foot to leave and the door flew open.

"Emily? What the hell are you doing here?"

Emily's eyes betrayed her and dipped down, past his chiseled jaw and tan skin to his wide pecs and bare abs, hard and toned to the point of causing her mouth to actually drop open.

Wow, oh fuck.

She'd never seen a man in real life as perfectly sculpted as Nathan was. He could model for any magazine cover and fit right in.

Fit is right.

"Hello? Did you hear me?"

Emily shook her head and forced herself to meet Nathan's eyes, the frown on his forehead severe and causing wrinkles on his otherwise perfect face.

"Ah, I…wanted to apologize for tonight."

He rolled his eyes at her. "You're kidding me? It's almost 1 a.m."

"I know, but I…" She looked up and down the hallway. "Can I come in for just a minute, and then I'll leave you alone. I promise."

Nathan stepped back and waved her in, his expression still grumpy.

Emily stepped inside, her eyes darting around the spacious lounge room filled with large, dark masculine furniture and no personal effects. Where were the photos or pictures on the walls? Even her toilet had quotes on the back of the door.

"Go on, then."

She turned back to him. His arms were crossed over his chest and her belly twisted into even tighter knots.

"Nathan, I know I shouldn't have pushed that on you tonight. It was wrong."

"It was. Especially when I specifically asked you not to."

"You did, and I'm very sorry."

He eyed her critically, his arms dropping down to his sides, exposing his smooth chest. "I suppose you're only here to beg for your job? I know how important it is to you."

She shook her head avidly, taking a step towards him. She needed him to understand it wasn't about that. "No. I don't care what you want to do about all that. We've spent time together lately and I feel like we've gotten to know each other a little. I shouldn't have done what I did."

Nathan's shoulders sagged. "You want a drink?"

"Ah, sure."

She could use one, a hot one preferably. Her hands were frozen and her lips were quivering.

"Red wine?"

Her eyebrows rose high as she followed him into the sterile, ultra-modern white kitchen. She should probably ask for a cup of tea, as this wasn't the atmosphere or the time of night for hot caffeine.

"Ah, sure. Why not?"

He didn't bother pulling on a shirt or shoes, just continued to walk around in faded blue jeans. The confidence he had was incredible.

Nathan stretched up and took down one red wine glass from a shelf in his fancy kitchen. The bulky muscles of his back and arms rippled and tightened as he moved. He opened the bottle and poured the alcohol, all with the grace of a leopard. The combination of strength and flexibility in his beautiful muscular frame as he moved around was hypnotizing to watch.

She slid onto one of the stools, her legs a little unsteady as warmth began to invade her lower belly. She'd known he was attractive, but by all that was holy, he was more beautiful than she'd realized.

He pushed a glass towards her and she took it, despite the fact that red wine was not on her list of favorite beverages. She'd make do tonight.

"Cheers." He tipped his glass of water towards her and drank without waiting for her to bring her own glass to his.

A shiver coursed through Emily. He was upset, and she wasn't sure what she could do to fix what she'd broken.

Despite needing that professional distance in the past, she was suddenly hating it now. A thin layer of ice seemed to have invaded the space between them and she didn't want it there.

"Nate, I am very sorry. I honestly thought that you'd love hearing the women's stories tonight. I assumed that if I pushed a little…"

"Yeah, you *assumed* and you know what they say about assumptions, right?"

She nodded. She certainly did. "Yeah, one of my dad's favorite expressions. If you 'assume' it makes an ass out of you and me."

He swallowed hard and stared at her with those striking blue eyes. "Yeah."

"You'd probably like my dad Nate, he's very pragmatic."

Nate shrugged and kept his eyes on his glass.

She didn't like her dad, but he was still around vaguely in the background of her life. She was pretty sure Nate wouldn't have the same answer if asked. "Do you and your dad get along?"

His head came up so fast she almost fell off her chair.

"That's none of your business, Emily."

"I'm sorry. So sorry. I didn't mean to pry. I just…" Hot tears stung at her eyes and she blinked rapidly, raising the glass to her lips and swallowing down the dry red with two big gulps. She was mucking everything up.

She got up and grabbed the bag that had slipped off her shoulder and onto the floor.

"Nate, Nathan. I…"

Two tears slipped down and she twisted away, holding her breath and trying to get her emotions under control. This was getting ridiculous.

She took one breath and then another, getting a handle on her feelings.

Enough. Stop.

She turned back around and gave Nathan a smile.

"I'm very sorry to have barged in on you like this. I just simply wanted to apologize for being intrusive and I hope you will forgive me and we can continue with our business relationship."

Nathan put his glass down, his eyes burning as he stared at her.

"How sorry are you, Emily?"

His tone was strangely erotic.

Confusing.

"Pardon?"

Nathan stalked forward and she backed up, the man in front of her grabbing around her waist and hauling her against his half-naked, muscled frame.

Her hands went to his chest, the hot skin burning her sensitive palms.

"Kiss me."

No.

8

———

"You know I can't do that. I work for you."

He gripped her harder. His strong fingers digging into her hips, sliding down her ass and pulling her so close the bulge in his jeans pressed hard against her belly.

He wanted her.

Oh God. Oh God. Oh God.

"I don't fucking care, Emmy. You came here tonight as a friend and I want you to be so much more. I've wanted you since the moment I saw you."

Emily lifted her eyes up to his, catching her bottom lip in her teeth. She wanted to give in so badly. But she didn't dare do as he asked.

His pupils dilated, making the bright blue of his irises almost disappear. His gaze dropped down to her lips as his hands tightened on her waist.

A growl rumbled from his lips and he swooped down, his hot mouth pressing against hers with a desperation she was unable to fight. He tasted like sweet heat and sexy male.

And he wanted her.

And she wanted him.

Her head swam, shutting down all logical protesting as her eyes closed, waves of pleasure flowing over her.

Nathan's tongue licked at the seam of her lips and she opened for him, unwilling and unable to fight him.

It had been so long since she'd been touched like this, and she ached for it so much. And it wasn't just anyone, it was him. Nate. The man she admired, lusted after.

One of his hands rose to cup her breast, his thumb skating across her nipple and pulling a moan from her. Hot arrows of desire flowed through her belly and below.

He pulled back and stared down at her as though asking an unspoken question.

She didn't reply with words, only let her lips kick up a little in a smile and he turned and pulled her by the hand through the living room and into the master suite.

His bedroom was the same as the rest of his house—modern, plain and masculine. The black covers and dark wooden bed was an imposing force in the room.

Nathan reached for her again, his warm lips finding the curve of her neck as his hands sought the zip on her dress.

Emily closed her eyes and let him undress her, her brain screaming out a warning just as her dress slithered to her feet.

"Damn, you're beautiful."

She didn't feel beautiful, hadn't in a very long time. She was too big, too inexperienced. What was she doing with a guy like him?

She crossed her arms over her breasts and turned around to face him.

"I'm so sorry, I shouldn't be doing this."

"Why not?"

"Because I'm not…"

"Not what?"

"Not beautiful, not fit, not what I'm sure you're used to having."

Nathan's chuckle made heat flood into her cheeks and she bent to grab her dress from the floor. How embarrassing! To have come so far only to be laughed at when she got down to her underwear.

His hands caught hers and drew her resisting form into his arms.

"You, Miss Emily, are bloody spectacular and I cannot wait to taste every inch of you. I'm going to make you scream and writhe and beg me to take you."

She gasped at him. "I wouldn't do that."

A sly smile spread across his lips that made her belly quiver.

"Wanna bet?"

She cocked her head at him, letting her body relax against him. "What do you have in mind?"

"Fifteen minutes and if you want to stop, then we're done."

That wasn't a lot of time. "Fifteen minutes to do what?"

"Anything I like."

Emily dug her fingernails into her palms, part of her desperate to do as he asked, the other part wishing she'd bothered to go to the gym and eat better. Her thighs were way too big!

"Come on, Emmy." His voice was smoothly cajoling and she lowered her eyebrows to glare at him.

He ignored her and took her hand again, pulling back the covers and motioning to her to lay down on his huge bed.

She did as she was told, lifting her legs and lying down on the soft sheets, watching his warm gaze as it roamed down her body.

She forced herself to keep her arms by her sides, despite the urge to cover up everything that was too round or fleshy.

"You have an incredible body. Don't change a single thing."

He rolled onto her and settled his huge weight between her thighs. She squeaked from the impact and he swooped down for another kiss, his tongue sweeping in to taste her.

Emily threw herself into the kiss, knowing there was nothing to lose now. There was something just so beautiful about the feel of his chest against hers. She ran her hands down his back, reveling in the large amounts of muscle beneath her palms and his smooth, hot skin. She may never get to be in Nate's bed ever again, and if she only had this one moment of insanity for the rest of her life, she was going to make it count.

He moaned while still kissing her, the sound going straight

through her and directly affecting her clit, the tiny pleasure button pulsing with hunger.

She lifted her legs and wrapped them around his denim-covered ass. He broke off their kiss, his lips trailing a path of fire down the side of her neck.

"Lift for me."

She arched up for him and he unclipped her bra with a practiced flick and tossed it onto the floor, her naked breasts now on display for him. She arched her back to press her breasts against his chest, the skin-to-skin contact making her insides turn to melted honey.

She looked into his face, searching for any signs of disgust but all she saw was a flash of hunger before he descended onto her nipples and sucked one into his mouth.

She gasped and threaded her fingers through his hair, closing her eyes as tendrils of pleasure fed through her belly, into her core.

His hands kneaded her breasts, plumping them up. His lips moved over to the other breast, her other nipple tightening as he ran his tongue around the pink areola and then touched the tip.

A moan escaped her and she pulled on his head to bring him closer. She needed more, she wanted to *feel* more.

His chuckle breathed against her skin as he slipped lower, kissing each inch of her belly as he moved back onto his haunches and tucked his hands into the sides of her knickers.

He lifted his eyes and held her gaze. She nodded her head just a fraction and he grinned at her as he slowly slipped her knickers down her legs. The lace whispered down her thighs and he threw them to the side, adding them to the growing pile of clothing on the floor.

She hadn't waxed or trimmed, but she kept herself relatively clean and…

Oh, shut up!

Nathan looked down between her thighs and licked his lips. She shivered and clenched her legs together. He shook his head and pressed her thighs apart, settling himself down between them on his belly.

She inhaled sharply and squealed as he extended his tongue and licked her clit. The heat and warmth of his mouth made her clamp her thighs together to contain the sensation. But he simply pressed them further apart, moaned and lifted his head to grin at her.

"You taste divine."

That would be impossible.

"I doubt that very much."

He chuckled again and ran his tongue from her opening up to her clit and moaned. "Well, you're wrong."

He winked once, then set his lips over her clit suckling on her until she cried out, pulses of pleasure seeping into her belly. He flicked his tongue over and over her sensitive nub, her pussy clenching tightly as heat flowed down the back of her legs.

She arched her spine, crying out as he worked on her and gave her more attention than any man ever had.

His finger circled her pussy opening and she found herself pressing down to gain the penetration, her starving body aching for him.

He didn't give it to her, though, simply spreading the moisture around and taunting her. His tongue lapped at her swollen clit, then delved down to taste her.

She screamed as her belly began to coil like a spring, her starved body craving the release he would soon give. She hoped. She prayed.

A groan exploded from her throat, and she dug her nails into his head as her orgasm built in her and she came in gripping waves of pleasure.

She cried out as the wave crested and then dropped, her belly shuddering and her legs tightening against him.

He pulled back and jumped up, standing next to her on the carpet.

Huh?

The heated wave flowed back and away, cold sand beneath her feet.

"What...?"

She sat up, her thighs slick with her own juices and her insides clawing at her with need.

"It's been fifteen minutes now. Are you staying?" Nathan toyed with the button on his jeans and relief flowed through her. He was just stopping to ask her if she wanted to keep going. She nodded emphatically.

No way was she leaving now.

He grinned and opened the fly on his jeans, pushing the denim down his strong legs and standing back up to reveal a slightly thickened cock and beautiful thighs.

She licked her lips and rolled onto her side, beckoning him closer with a look she hoped said everything she was feeling inside.

HER SWEET TASTE was still on his lips and his eyes couldn't decide which pair of delicious pink lips they wanted to stare at most.

She was too perfect, and so different from any other woman he'd ever had in his bed. Her curves were larger, her passion more honest. She made his breath catch and his gut tighten. And he wasn't sure he could walk away from this woman as easily as he had everyone else.

"Nate?" Her voice had a question in it. She was cooling down and he didn't want that.

No more thinking.

"Open your legs for me and show me how beautiful you are."

He began stroking his cock, watching her as she did as he asked, lying on his bed and showing him her beautiful body.

He moved to the end of the bed and stared at her. "Anything you want to show me?"

She sat up and slid to the end of the bed. "Can I touch you?"

"Ah, yeah." He took his cock and offered it to her. He couldn't really get hard for anyone anymore. He'd let her suck him for a minute, then turn her over and fix himself before he entered her.

She looked up at him with wide eyes. "How do you like it? Will you teach me?"

"Pardon?"

She shrugged. "I don't have a lot of experience and I want to please you."

No one had ever said anything like that to him before. Ever. Women took from him. Lay back and let him do what he wanted to get them to come. They didn't care about what he liked.

It was the main reason he couldn't get hard easily anymore. He was rarely inspired by some female wanting to use him as though he were a talented dildo.

"I love strong suction, a little teeth. And look at me."

She grinned and opened her mouth, encircling him with one long suck. Heat flowed through him and when she looked up, his balls pulsed with desire.

He grabbed the back of her head and guided her to glide up and down his length until she got the rhythm and he had to pull away, the tingles of his orgasm teasing at the base of his spine.

"Sorry. Did I do it wrong?"

He groaned and touched himself again. "No, that was perfect. I had to pull away or I was going to come right then. Roll over."

She frowned at him but did as she was told, flipping onto her knees and opening her legs for him.

Her ass was round and firm and as he stepped over to the bedside table to grab some protection, he admired the strength in her body.

"You really are beautiful, Emmy. Spectacular, actually."

She looked his way and grimaced. "I don't know how you can say that."

He stepped behind her and tapped her ass with the hard length of his cock. "This here doesn't lie sweetheart, and in this position, you are perfection."

He ran his hands over the outside of her smooth thighs, up her ass and along her spine.

She bumped back against him and a growl rumbled through his chest.

He took his cock and pressed it against her pink opening, thrusting his hips once, twice, then breaching the entrance.

"Ah..." She gasped and pressed back against him, so he slid in deep, letting her hot, tight body take him in completely.

Nate groaned and tightened his belly to stop himself coming too quickly. "Fuck, you feel amazing."

"You. Do. Too."

Her hand slid back and gripped his fingers where they held her hip, the connection she was trying to make so simple it hit him in the chest like a rib tackle. She knew who he was, she wanted him close.

She wants a connection to me. Wow.

He shook his head and began to ride her, concentrating on the rhythm, the strokes. Trying not to get too caught up in what this was, what it meant to either of them.

She moaned beneath him, tossing her head and pushing back against him as he thrust harder and faster.

Her body squeezed him like a glove, a perfectly formed, tight, hot glove.

"Nate… Oh God… Nate." His name on her lips was perfect and he was beginning to slip. She was so sexy, so honest, so warm and tender.

Heat tickled up his spine and tightened his balls. This was all happening too fast, but she felt so good, so perfect beneath his hands and around his cock. He thrust again and her pussy squeezed him so tightly he let go of all control.

"I'm coming… fuuu...ck." He pumped into her once more and she gripped his hand tight.

Fire poured through his body and he cried out, his cock spasming inside her.

His head exploded and white light fizzled around him.

When he came back to reality, she was stroking his thigh and he was still inside her.

She was too close. The cold was creeping into his belly super-fast this time. Fear, like a snake coiling inside him, ready to attack.

He needed to break away before he said something he'd regret.

"I'll be back in a minute."

He withdrew, his cock slipping out into the cold and he wanted to thrust straight back into her warmth.

Stop it. You sound like a pussy.

"Are you okay?" she asked, her body now sliding down into a prone position, her face soft and relaxed as she stared at him.

"Yeah, I'm just a bit sweaty. Gotta rinse quick."

"Okay, Nate."

He walked away to his ensuite, wiping away the condom and throwing it in the bin and grabbed the face washer, wetting it and wiping himself.

Wow. That was a little too good.

He looked himself in the mirror and stared himself down. The reflection shocked him. His eyes were drugged, his hair mussed and standing on end.

He took a sniff of himself and moaned as their combined smells met his nose. Sex and sweat…cum. The most earthy smell around.

He couldn't go back in there or he'd just fuck her again. There was something intoxicating about the way she responded to him, her enthusiasm for him was so authentic. So genuine.

He reached into the shower and turned on the taps, hot water blasting out of the silver head and making him jump back.

He glanced back at the closed door.

She could probably use a shower too.

No. Get on with it.

If he had a shower without her she'd hopefully get the point and leave, then he wouldn't have to kick her out.

He groaned as he stepped beneath the hot spray, water beating down on his shoulders and infiltrating his tense muscles.

"Ahhh…" He turned and tilted his head back, letting the water wash away the evidence of what he'd done with one of his solicitors and the stress of the day, which had mostly been there because of her.

Nathan turned off the water and dried himself, his ears not picking up any signs of movement from the bedroom.

Get yourself together. You barely know this girl. Stop feeling things.

The sensation of her hand on his still lingered, the sounds of her hot moans in his ears. She was amazing. It was all incredible.

And he'd end it now.

Before it became something more. Before she got into his heart and he didn't know himself anymore. He'd worked too hard for too long to be who he was, and a woman like Emily was the sort who could be his undoing.

He'd felt it.

The crack in his armor the moment her hand had touched his.

And it stops now.

The weakness, the softness in him that she exposed was almost painful. He didn't want it, or her influence in his life. No matter how good it felt in the short term, long term it would only bring havoc, for her and especially for him.

He wrapped the towel around his waist and opened the door. He clenched his fists and walked back into his bedroom.

"Emily…"

Nate frowned and walked forward, keeping a firm hand on the knot of his towel.

His words bounced around the quiet room, the sound of her even breathing reaching him over the space between her sleeping form and him.

He walked up to his side of the bed and stared at her face. She'd lain down on her side and pulled up the blanket.

He sighed and let his eyes wander over her. Her thick eyelashes fanned out on her cheeks and her soft lips were parted, still swollen and red from his kisses.

Nathan stepped back and cleared his throat as he glanced around his room and weighed his options. He had a guest bedroom but the mattress left a lot to be desired. His bed was a king and he was sure he wouldn't even know she was there if she stayed on the edge like she currently was.

He groaned and ran a hand through his hair. He didn't share his bed with anyone. It built an intimacy he didn't want, gave them the wrong impression and he didn't *want* to hurt anyone. Especially not someone like her.

He could wake her up.

His eyes travelled over the expanse of creamy skin of her shoulders and breasts, her rounded hips and long legs. All that beauty, and she looked so tired. She worked as hard as he did, which was an incredible thing to admit.

No, waking her wasn't an option.

What other choice did he now have? He strolled over to his chest of drawers and dropped the towel on the ground. He'd get a good night's sleep, hopefully, and then tell her to go home in the morning. No point making a scene now.

He pulled on some cotton boxers and strolled back to the bed, climbing in with a grin tugging up the sides of his lips.

She sighed softly and his eyes closed, her soft breathing somehow reassuring in the darkness.

He tapped the bedside lamp and everything fell quiet.

9

———

a light snoring snuck into Emily's dreams in the form of a cat, sitting next to her phone breathing like a grandpa.

That didn't make sense.

She frowned as she woke, stretching her arms up and groaning as her muscles ached through her legs and ass.

Her eyes popped open as the sheets moved over her naked breasts. She looked down and grabbed the blankets.

Why the hell was she naked?

She twisted to the side and froze, Nathan Johnson's light snoring form before her.

The night before came crashing in like a tidal wave.

Her coming over to his apartment, his offer that had been too good to refuse. The incredible sex that had followed… and…had he left her?

She looked around.

Oh crap, I just fell asleep.

After. We. Had. Amazing. Sex.

She lay back against the pillows and put a hand to her forehead.

How the hell was she going to fix this one?

The snoring had ceased and she slowly turned her head to the side,

Nate's bright blue eyes stared back at her. He looked confused for a moment, then he frowned.

She spoke first. "Good morning."

"Oh. Hey."

His throat was thick and husky with the morning as he rolled onto his back and stretched just as she had.

They were only inches apart and as Emily took her arms out from under the blankets and lay them on top of the coverlet, she could see red finger marks from where he must have held her during her sleep.

Her bladder began to throb and beg her to stand up and go to the toilet, the pressure making her clench her legs together.

"Ah, I need to go to the toilet."

Nate grinned at her, though his eyes were cold.

"Ensuite is through there." He pointed at an open door off the bedroom and she glanced back at him. He couldn't be serious?

He chuckled again, putting his arms behind his head in a classic show of masculine smugness.

"What's wrong with you? It's not like I haven't seen it all before."

Heat washed over Emily's face and prickled her scalp. After everything they'd done last night, why did standing naked before him now feel dirty? She set her jaw and flung back the covers.

Cold air pierced her warm and naked skin like a thousand needles, yet she was too angry to do anything other than jump up and grab her clothes from the floor.

What happened between last night and this morning?

She stomped to the bathroom and slammed the door, her heart banging against her ribs as she breathed hard and fast.

That bloody wanker! How had she been so stupid as to fall for his charms last night? And what was with the ice treatment this morning?

Hot, angry tears filled her eyes and she dashed them away with hands that shook.

What a horrible, stupid mistake.

Enough.

She blew out a breath and took another, closing her eyes to calm herself.

So she'd had her first one-night stand, and it had been with one of her clients. No big deal.

Yeah, right.

She dropped her clothes on the white wash basin and turned on the shower. No point rushing back out into a bedroom when Dr. Jekyll was out again.

She adjusted the temperature to slightly too hot and stepped beneath the scalding spray, washing every inch of her with soap, aiming to rid herself of the night before.

He hadn't been inside her without a condom on, luckily. She wasn't on any type of birth control and hadn't been aware enough last night to really care at the time. He had, thankfully.

A sob rose in her throat and she let it free, letting the water wash it away, too. *How can something that was so beautiful and felt so good, turn into something so weird and bad?*

Maybe she was overreacting? She had a history of misreading Nate and she could be doing it right now.

Okay. Pull yourself together.

She stepped out of the shower, toweled herself dry and put her party clothes back on. It felt cheap but she tried not to judge herself too much.

This was a first.

She looked in the mirror and attempted to arrange her hair into a semblance of normality.

Time to face the music.

She opened the door again and found him gone.

"Nathan?"

"In the kitchen."

She walked out of the bedroom and stepped into the pristine apartment, expecting a smile. Anything.

Instead, there was a man in sports gear taping his hands for boxing, or something like it.

"Um… Thank you for last night, Nathan."

He winked at her in a crude way. "No problem, babe."

She stared at him for a moment, waiting for his expression to change or for him to offer her a coffee, a glass of water even.

But the silence stretched on and he continued to tape his knuckles.

"I suppose I'll go then."

"Yeah. See you at work, probably."

"Yeah. Probably."

She grabbed her bag and ran from his apartment, her head spinning and her chest aching. How many personalities did this one guy have?

Monday morning was usually one of his favorite moments of the week. Normally, anyway.

"Good morning, Mr. Johnson." Martine chirped at him as he slunk past her desk and entered his office. His head throbbed like a motherfucker.

The door clicked shut just as he got to his chair and dropped into it.

"What's up your ass this morning?"

He rolled his eyes at the woman who, if he was completely honest, was one of his best friends.

"Nothing you haven't seen before, Martine, I'm sure."

The blonde woman who oversaw everything behind the scenes of his company stepped forward and ran a keen eye over him.

"I'm really not in the mood for you this morning." He looked up at her quickly, then glanced down at the file he'd placed on his desk Friday night before leaving.

Martine frowned harder, pursing her glossy lips in a way he hadn't seen for years.

"I'm calling in my birthday favor."

A groan vibrated through his vocal chords before he could properly stop himself.

No. Anything but that.

He forced a smile to his lips and leaned back in his chair.

"Oh, come on. You can have anything you want with that birthday wish. A flight to Paris? A week in Hawaii?"

"Oh, now I know this is good." She stepped around the chair opposite him and dropped into it, crossing her skinny legs and raising one eyebrow. "If you'd rather pay thousands of dollars for me to have a holiday than answer a question, then I know what I want."

He rolled his eyes heavenward and blew out a nice, long breath. Martine knew him better than anyone in the world and he wished she'd just take the money rather than ask him this one thing.

"What's your question? You only get one."

He stared at her and waited, hoping she'd stuff up the delivery so he could at least hide behind the answer.

"Nathan. Why are you in such a foul mood? Does it have anything to do with Eleanor's House anniversary on Saturday night? You better not leave out any details."

He sighed and shrugged his shoulders, a strange swirling in his belly heralding a nervousness he rarely felt.

"I'm grumpy because I had a shit night's sleep last night, and yes, my mood may have been affected by Saturday night."

Martine gestured with her hands to go on and he clenched his jaw. He'd answered the question she wanted, but something tugged at him to continue. He trusted Martine more that anyone and he wanted to say it out loud. The confusion about the other night was eating him alive.

"I went to the anniversary night with Emily. Well, not *with* her, but..." Martine's eyebrows shot up and he glanced away, not wanting to even discuss the look he was seeing in her eyes.

"When you say you went, do you mean you took her home with you afterwards? Why would that put you in such a foul mood?"

He couldn't answer that.

"Nathan." Her tone was strict, hard. A schoolteacher's. "Even when sex is bad, it's still pretty good. What could she have done to put you in a mood like this?"

He picked up his pen and tapped it against his desk. "Honestly,

Martine, I have no idea. It was good, but then she stayed, and I wanted her gone, but afterwards I just felt crap."

"You let her get close to you, then kicked her out?"

He nodded, letting his eyes lose focus as they stared at the blank computer screen.

"Nathan Johnson, you're a pretty smart man. If you can't work out what's wrong with that equation, something's malfunctioning in your brain."

Nothing wrong here. I just don't wanna feel like this.

Nathan swung around in his chair and stared out the window, the noise of his door opening and then clicking shut again echoing in the large room.

He was alone again. How he liked it. How he was used to it.

The beautiful city skyline outside his window blurred as his eyes shifted focus and his brain went over his Sunday.

Emily had jumped in his shower when he'd goaded her into using the ensuite. He'd stayed in bed, his body throbbing with pain as he imagined her beneath the hot water.

She had the most delicious nipples and pussy. Everything about a woman's body that could turn him off if they weren't well appointed, she had in perfect spades.

The smell of her was... A moan escaped him as his cock had swelled beneath the covers as he lay there in bed.

But he'd refused his body's cries for more sex and left her alone. He had only one choice when it came to the testosterone pumping through his bloodstream, and that had been to train.

He'd hauled himself out of bed and readied himself for boxing.

She'd entered the kitchen ten minutes later, dressed and pressed and thanked him for a great night with as much warmth as an icicle on a ski slope.

He had to admit that he probably hadn't been as cordial as he could have been, either.

When she'd finally left his apartment, the normal relief he felt when his lovers finally left him alone was missing. Instead, a gaping loneliness settled into his huge home.

He'd spent his Sunday as he normally did. A bit of work, training, some football and take away.

Sleep evaded him on any normal night but he'd struggled to get to sleep before 2 a.m. and when he realized it was probably because he'd had close to seven hours sleep the night before, he'd practically keeled over.

He never slept more than three hours and a lot of the dark hours of the night were filled with torturous nightmares or wide-awake memories that made it impossible to sleep.

How had he slept so long beside Emily?

How had she kept the demons away?

He didn't sleep beside his lovers often, but no one had ever come close to giving him such peace.

He'd spent the rest of the night trying to solve the puzzle, finally passing out around 5 a.m.

Nathan swiveled around in his chair once again and turned on his computer. It was time to get into work.

"EMILY, there's a phone call on line two for you."

Emily blinked and pulled herself away from her computer screen, a phone call? Huh?

"Who is it?"

No one called anymore. All of her clients emailed her and the hundreds of emails in her inbox since this morning testified to that.

"It's Nathan Johnson."

Except *him* of course. Her stomach dropped away so fast she gasped out loud. She'd ignored the email from Martine on Monday and the email from him on Tuesday.

She'd emailed Martine back this morning to say she'd be in on Friday for a few hours, but she knew it wasn't enough. If they didn't reprimand her at the very least for her lack of focus on them, she'd be very surprised.

Her gaze flickered down to the flashing light on line two.

Shit.

She reached out and picked up the phone, pressing the button that would connect Nathan with her once again.

She forced chirpiness into her voice that she was not feeling.

"Hello, Emily speaking."

"Hello, Emily."

A shiver coursed through her body, making her literally shake. His tones were like pure silk, rich and expensive.

"Mr. Johnson, how can I help you?"

She picked up a pen and began tapping it against the desk, a distraction to her eyes as she tried to force the heat from her cheeks. Four days ago she'd been naked and beneath the man with whom she was speaking, and she wasn't quite sure how to react.

"You can come into the office today and finish the contract you started last week."

His tone was harsh and it brought with it a good dose of cold reality. She straightened in her chair and the warmth in her cheeks leeched from her face.

"I'm sorry but my schedule is booked up today, Mr. Johnson. I could reschedule some things tomorrow if it's urgent."

She waited, the terse breathing on the end of the line making her bite her lip. He could fire her, but then she'd be relieved. So what was she worried about?

"Fine. Schedule a time with Martine and we'll see you then."

The line went dead and she looked down at the receiver. She wasn't quite sure what had just happened.

Carefully placing the handset back into its cradle, she attempted to ignore the whirl of puzzle pieces flying around in her head. She'd tried so hard during the week not to over-analyze what had happened on the weekend, putting it down to a momentary lapse of judgement that had resulted in some pretty spectacular sex.

Of course, she'd expected nothing less from a man like him—worldly, charming and very experienced. But his brush-off after the fact had seemed harsh and over the top.

He'd treated her like a classic one-night-stand piece of trash on Sunday morning, not that she'd ever experienced it before, but it didn't take a genius to work out the routine. After that, she'd expected him to keep their contact to a minimum, not contact her twice in a few days.

He wanted her back in his workspace again. But why?

She couldn't have judged him wrongly again, could she?

She shook her head and got back into work mode. There was only one way to find out.

"Martine, coffee please."

Nathan kept his head down and didn't stop drawing, knowing that his executive assistant didn't necessarily like fetching his coffee, but she'd do it if asked politely.

A minute or two later a steaming mug was placed down on the desk in front of him.

"Thank you."

He didn't look up, just kept his eyes on his work and ignored the clawing ache in his legs.

Emily was here and he wanted to see her. But he wouldn't. He absolutely refused to. She was only one of the solicitors working for his company and although Saturday night had been good—fucking hot, actually—he didn't want to repeat it.

Of course, you do! Don't fucking lie to yourself.

A knock sounded on his door and he jumped. Emily stuck her head around the door.

"I'm sorry to interrupt, Mr. Johnson, but I have one question to ask you."

Oh, damn. This isn't going to be as easy as I thought.

"Please come in." He waved to her and grabbed his mug, taking a slurp of dark, rich coffee. Heat spread through his belly, that familiar buzz of caffeine travelling through his body.

He sighed as he placed it down again, his eyes devouring the woman in front of him. She was dressed very starkly today. Black shirt, black skirt, hair tied back into a low bun.

Was she trying to look ugly? Because she severely underestimated his memory if she was trying to turn him off. He knew how smooth her skin was beneath that outfit, how perfectly curved her ass and hips were. Nothing would ever disguise that from him again.

Emily stood before him and held a file across her chest like a life vest.

"There is something in this file that doesn't make sense. One of the new contracts seems to have slipped in some excessive extra fees, and I wanted to make sure you agreed to them before I sent them off for you to sign."

"Pardon? Show me."

Emily slid the file across the desk, the section she was speaking about marked with sticky notes and question marks.

"I've been over a lot of your past contracts to get a feel for what's normal for your business, and this seems excessive."

Excessive is right!

He'd never seen so many hidden fees in one place before. She'd just saved him a small fortune.

"It's highway robbery is what it is! You did a brilliant job of picking this up, Emily. Thank you. I'll sort it out from here."

He smiled at her and placed the file next to the phone. He'd do more than sort that one out. He'd never work with that construction company again.

Emily gave him a nod and began to back away. His belly clenched and his breath caught in his throat.

No. Stop!

"Emily, we should talk about Saturday night."

"No." She practically fired the word at him, then shook her head and stared at the ground, red highlighting her high cheekbones.

"I mean about Eleanor's House. I believe I may have over-reacted to what you said to everyone."

She stopped backing away and glanced up, her eyes bright and wary.

Something twisted deep in his chest. He swallowed hard.

"No, I was wrong to push you, Nate. I know I was. Whatever happened, I take responsibility for."

He shrugged and let his lips lift into a semblance of a smile. He was giving her an apology and an out, and she wasn't taking it. He liked that.

"Well, let's forget about it and you can tell me more about your career aspirations over dinner."

"Oh. No, Nate, we shouldn't."

He chuckled and stood up, rounding his desk and heading towards her. He didn't stop when she gasped and jumped away from him, just kept moving forward, reaching out to shut the door and looked directly at her for the first time.

"Oh, I'm Nate again, am I?"

She softly whacked him on the chest. "Stop it, you know what I mean."

"No, what do you mean?"

She glared at him, the fire that he so loved about her, returning. "I mean we can't go out for dinner again."

"Why not?"

"Because you're my client and it would be inappropriate."

He heaved a sigh and stuck both hands into his trouser pockets. Those same excuses were not going to fly with him now. He'd tasted her lips, held her body through the best night's sleep he'd had in decades and he missed her. He couldn't continue like this.

"Emmy, seriously, let's be done with the excuses. You volunteered at my charity for years before you came to work here officially, and you know there are no laws to say we can't have dinner, or even sleep together if it comes to that."

"It won't come to that again. Not after what happened last time."

He grinned at her, ignoring the last remark. "Don't go laying down rules just yet, okay?"

She heaved a huge sigh, her shoulders going up, and then settling much lower. "Nate, why do you want to have dinner with me?"

"The truth?"

"Always."

Something lurched inside his belly once again and he stared at Emily, her clear, brown eyes as honest as a child's. He wasn't sure where she got her optimism from, but he wanted some of it.

"I have to ask you something first. Are you a bitch underneath all of these bright-eyed smiles and goody-two-shoe behavior?"

She took a step back, her lower lip actually quivering a little.

"No! Don't get upset. Look, the reason I ask is, the only woman I ever got close to caring about went from sunshine and roses one minute, to an utter abusive bitch the next. I've never met a woman who didn't, and I need you to tell me now if it's going to happen, and I'll be prepared for it."

He stared at her, watching the pain flicker across her face as she swallowed and shook her head. "I'm sorry to disappoint you but, no. I'm not a bitch. Never have been, never will be."

"Good." He heaved a theatrical sigh of relief and gave her a smile. Nerves flickered in his belly and something was crawling over the back of his neck. Fear this old and ingrained was not going to disappear anytime soon, but he wasn't willing to walk away from her just yet.

"Em, I want to get to know you. You're beautiful, kind and funny. A combination I have never even remotely seen before, and I'm sick of finding excuses why we shouldn't get to know each other better."

Her eyes widened and glistened for a moment before she blinked and glanced away. "Okay."

He straightened up and grabbed the door handle.

"Let's go, then."

"But it's only six o'clock."

He shrugged and held the door open. He owned the business. What was the problem?

"Good, then we'll have time to talk before bed."

Her cheeks flushed pink and he laughed as she glared and shuffled off towards her office. Warmth filled his chest, his shoulders expanding and growing with strength.

He had her again, for tonight.

"Oh, Nathan," Martine called out to him, her voice impregnated with laughter.

He stopped and turned, Martine's giggle catching his attention.

"Leaving so soon?"

He couldn't stop the corners of his mouth lifting up.

"Time to get some dinner."

She walked over to his door and grabbed the handle, shutting it with a concise click. She nodded at him once and gave him an approving smile.

"See you in the morning."

He turned away as Emily came walking back, lightness inside his chest making him grin far too much.

"Hey, what's so funny?" Emily asked as they walked towards the elevators.

He shook his head. "Nothing. Just Martine being her normal self."

"And what's that?"

"Someone who knows me far too well."

10

———

Emily couldn't believe how quickly dinner flew by, which was very unusual for them. They somehow managed to stick to topics of work and the weather, thus stopping any possible fight.

Soon, they were walking outside once again and Nate reached over and grabbed her hand. She jumped a little at the contact, but soon settled to it, her arm tingling from awareness.

She linked her fingers with his and stepped closer, not fighting him when he pulled her to him once again.

"Come home with me."

"We need to talk about last Saturday night first."

He groaned and rolled his eyes. "Do we need to ruin the night already?"

"That's not fair." She glared at him and he finally laughed.

"Okay. What about it?"

She took a breath and squeezed his hand. These questions had tortured her all day Sunday, her anger towards him the only thing stopping her from crying over the whole thing.

"You obviously didn't hate it, or you wouldn't be wanting to repeat the experience."

He groaned and stopped her in their tracks, swooping down to kiss her hard and fast. "It was hot and very memorable. I couldn't get you out of my mind for days. I had to make you come back into work."

Come on, give me a little bit more than that.

"So you could…"

"Talk you back into my bed."

She rolled her eyes and pulled on his hand to keep on walking. He tugged her back, wrapping his arms around her properly, embracing her there on the street for everyone to see.

"You want more. Okay, look. I woke up the next morning and didn't handle it that well. I know I practically threw you out—and I shouldn't have."

Wow. I think that's almost an apology.

"But that doesn't mean the night wasn't amazing, or you weren't a beautiful lover. I don't have much experience dealing with those sorts of situations and wasn't quite sure what to do."

"So you just got up and decided to start a workout?"

He pressed a soft kiss to her lips again, then shrugged. "That was what I always do on a Sunday morning. I find comfort in my routine."

She squeezed his biceps. "Me, too."

Should she really let him off the hook that easily? "But what about all the other women who have slept over?"

He narrowed his eyes at her. "What other women? No one's slept beside me in fifteen odd years. I don't let people stay, but you—"

"But with me?"

He grinned. "You fell asleep and you were so beautiful on that pillow. I didn't want to wake you up."

Her heart tugged at his words. She wasn't sure that was enough. She wanted so much more, but for now, she'd have to take it. He hadn't woken her up and kicked her out, instead choosing to sleep beside her and cuddle her all night. That had to mean something.

Didn't it?

"Okay, then."

"Okay, what?"

"I'll come home with you tonight."

Nate opened his mouth as though to fight her on it, and then obviously registered what she said. The smile he gave her was worth putting her fears aside.

His Jekyll and Hyde routine had to be due to his childhood, or his mother's death. Something made him switch from warmth to ice in seconds, and if she could get closer to him, she could try to help him, heal him. Maybe love him enough that he might trust her.

"Great. My car's parked back near work."

They hurried back to his tiny black sports car and she got in while shaking her head.

"What's wrong?"

She giggled and motioned to his car.

"Don't they say guys with sports cars are trying to compensate for something—and you don't have that problem."

She gave him a huge smile and he laughed, the stress lines she usually saw around his eyes smoothing out. "Why, thank you, ma'am."

They drove the two minutes back to his apartment and held hands as they rode the elevator up to the third floor. It felt right coming home with him. She'd be a loser if she slept with him and he didn't respect her.

They had a long way to go, but she was beginning to see that there was a lot more to this man than met the eye.

As soon as the front door shut, their arms wrapped around one another with a hunger she hadn't expected. Her heart thumped against her breast, his breathing ragged in the room.

This time, they made love with no words, no fancy moves or sexy foreplay. He slipped inside her and lay on top, kissing her deeply, staying close, heart to heart, until they climaxed together in a shower of moans.

As she began drifting off to sleep, her body sated and her heart strangely full, she snuggled back into his warmth. His hand landed on her hip as he tugged her to him.

"It's all right if I stay, isn't it?"

It was a weekday and she'd have to haul ass in the morning to get home, change and get back to work on time, but there was no way she was leaving him after what they'd just shared.

He didn't answer and she twisted around to stare at him. He had his eyes closed and a strange frown on his face. She wanted to stay, but she may not have a choice.

"What's wrong?"

He shook his head and glanced at her. "Nothing. Of course, you can stay."

He looked down, his eyes shadowed even in the dark. There was something so sad about him, tortured.

She reached up a hand and cupped his cheek.

"Hey, you can tell me if you don't want me to stay. I'll be a bit upset, but I don't want to impose on you."

When he didn't respond again a lead-like vise wrapped around her heart and squeezed. She must have been alone in her delusion of a blossoming romance.

"All right, I'll go." She made to get up and his arm snaked out and pulled her back against his solid chest so fast, the breath oomphed out of her.

"No. I want you to stay."

He held tight, wrapping both arms around her. She couldn't help smiling as she settled back against him.

"Good night, Nate. Thank you for tonight."

"Good night, beautiful girl."

Emmy awoke to an electronic alarm, contented snoring in her ear and a hot male body pressed against her back. They'd barely moved since falling asleep.

She reached out and turned off her alarm, Nate rolling onto his back and stretching like a cat.

"Good morning," she said as she turned and snuggled into him, holding onto the hope that he wouldn't turn on her this morning as he had the other time.

He kissed her on top of the head and wrapped his arms around her.

"Good morning, beautiful."

She squeezed tightly as her breath hitched in her throat and unshed tears stung her eyes.

Oh, thank you.

"What time is it?" he asked, his throat thick with sleep.

"Before seven. I have to rush home and get some new clothes before work so I better head out."

"Seven? Are you kidding me?"

She raised her head. "No, why?"

He stared at her for a minute and then laughed, rolling on top of her and settling between her open thighs like he was meant to be there.

"Hey." She pushed playfully at his chest, although she wasn't really trying to push him off. His weight felt so perfect on top of her. His bulk a comfort, his heat perfect for nestling into. "I was trying to get up."

"Do you know that I haven't slept past sunrise since I was a teenager? You're some awesome sleep aid."

She rolled her eyes as his lips descended, kissing her neck and moving south to her breasts. "Thanks for the compliment."

He must have heard her sarcastic tone and looked up with a confused expression in his eyes. "I'm serious. You feel like home."

They both froze at that moment and he pulled back, rolling off her to stand up and move towards the bathroom.

"Ah, just going to use the toilet. Back soon."

He disappeared and she sat up, holding the sheets to her breasts.

You feel like home.

No words had ever sounded sweeter. Not any "I love you" from her parents, not false compliments from past lovers. In four words Nathan had described everything that was important, and she never wanted to lose that.

She stared at the closed bathroom door and sighed heavily. He was running from her and how he felt about her, and she understood that.

You didn't get to be Nathan's age and still be single without carrying a decent amount of baggage or scars.

His mother had suffered physical abuse at the hands of his father, she knew that. That in itself was enough to set most people on the path to rocky relationships.

She slipped her legs off the bed and stepped over to the bathroom.

"Hey, Nate. I better head off soon. Can I use your shower quickly?"

He opened the door with a smile. "Yeah sure, but you don't need to run home. There's a shop in the foyer that has some beautiful suits that would look amazing on you. They open at eight."

She looked down at the tiled bathroom floor. "Thanks, but I really can't afford anything new."

He slid an arm around her waist and tilted her chin up. "Yeah, well I can. They have my details and I'll call down to instruct to put it on my account."

She frowned as different sides of her personality warred in her head. She didn't want to be bought. She wasn't a hooker. Images of Pretty Woman flashed through her head.

"When's your birthday?"

She glanced up at him at the change of topic. "Third of December." Which was a month away.

"How about the suit can be your birthday present, then?"

"That's a very expensive birthday present, Nate." She could feel herself softening as her hands slid up his bare arms and moved around his neck.

"Then make it a Christmas present, too."

She weighed her next words carefully, but decided she'd push through the barrier despite the possible repercussions.

"That's even further away. You sure we'll still know each other then?"

His eyes grew shuttered and he kissed her lightly on the lips. "I'm sure we will, and even if we don't, I want you to have breakfast with me, so I'll buy you a suit and you can stay."

She nodded before she thought better of it. It would be stupid to throw the offer back in his face, especially since it meant he wanted her to stay with him as long as possible. Sure, he wasn't exactly making the declarations of intent that she would like, but one step at a time.

"What's for breakfast, then?"

TWO HOURS, one omelet, two showers, and another hot lovemaking session later, she was walking into her office slightly warmer than the weather called for.

"Wow, nice suit! Where'd you get that?"

Emily shuffled into her desk space, plopped down her laptop and briefcase and slid into her seat.

Kristy came barreling around the corner.

"Tell me, tell me!"

Emily frowned at her designer-loving friend as she carefully took out her laptop and turned it on.

"It's new, nothing special."

"You're kidding me? Have you finally decided to spend some money on clothes? I am so impressed, Em! You look amazing."

Emily shook her head at her friend and shooed her away. Meanwhile, the heat in her cheeks had reached the point where she was shrugging out of her designer jacket to cool down.

Why did someone have to notice straight away?

A wolf whistle sounded behind her and she ignored it.

Kristy sent her an email that tinged in her inbox.

Hot blouse too!

Emily couldn't stop the giggle that rose and she twisted in her chair and stuck her tongue out at Kristy.

It was a beautiful ensemble the woman had chosen for her.

A sky blue blouse and a navy pinstriped suit that accentuated her small waist and did nothing to hide her large breasts. She looked businesslike, but very feminine. Not a style she ever thought she'd be able to afford, or have the guts to wear. But after a night with Nate and a very persuasive sales assistant, she now owned a very beautiful suit.

This morning had been so very different from last Sunday morning. The whole experience had been so much more deeply satisfying. The sex on Saturday night had been hot, but last night had been better somehow. She woke up feeling loved, treasured, wanted by him. If that was her delusion, she'd own it when it came down to it, but for the moment, she was living the dream.

She set to work and around lunchtime she received a phone call she hadn't quite expected.

"Hello, beautiful, how's your day been?"

She giggled as she answered, the response totally inappropriate, but she couldn't stop it.

"Great, how about yours?"

"Busy, but good. What are you laughing about?"

She bit her lip as she jiggled in her chair. "Nothing, I'm just happy you called."

"Good."

There was a comfortable silence and Emily decided to jump into the gap.

"Do you want to come over to my house tonight? I won't finish until late, but we could probably watch a movie, or something."

His low chuckle on the end of the line signaled the fact that he understood her message. Another night like last night was definitely on the cards for her. She was addicted to his kisses and craved those feelings that only he could give her.

"Sure. I can swing by and pick you up at eight if you like?"

"Perfect!"

She hung up, smiling. Finally, a man who would understand the long hours she kept and her passion for her work.

Her night, unfortunately, didn't work out the way she'd planned.

At six o'clock she received a phone call that her mother had been hospitalized and she dropped everything to run to her side.

Her work granted her a few days off and she rang Nathan to apologize as she was packing up.

"I am so sorry to cancel on you, but I have to go. Mum's in the hospital and I'll need to stay with her for a few days."

"Ah, all right. Where does she live?"

"About four hours' drive north, a small town near Swan Hill. I really have to run, but call me if you can. I'll have my mobile phone with me."

"No. I'll let you concentrate. Call me when you get back."

"All right, and again, I'm sorry."

"No, don't be. These things happen."

They hung up and Emily could not shake the strongest feeling that something was wrong. She hoped it wasn't her mum.

She drove straight to Swan Hill Hospital, exhausted but safe as she pulled into the car park close to 10 p.m.

They had a small emergency ward and she entered through that door.

"Can I help you?"

"Yes. I've driven up from Melbourne to see my mother. She was brought into the Emergency Room this afternoon."

"Visiting hours aren't open until ten o'clock in the morning now."

She stared at the woman for a moment and took a deep breath. "I have driven four hours to check on how my mother is doing. I can go back to her house tonight, but I need to know if she is okay. Will you please check with someone so that I can have an update on her status?"

The snotty receptionist stood up and stuck out her huge breasts.

"And do you have sufficient evidence that you are indeed related to the patient?"

Emily placed the paperwork she always carried in her car on the bench.

"My birth certificate, copies of my driver's license and Medicare card. A copy of my mother's enduring medical power of attorney."

The receptionist snorted, took the file and disappeared for a few minutes.

Emily jumped up and down on the spot for a moment, encouraging the blood to pump through her body. She was so mentally wired still, but her body was exhausted. She hated sitting in a car for so long. One of the main reasons she didn't visit her mum as often as she should.

A male doctor returned with the nurse.

"Emily Sanders?"

"Yes, that's me."

"You mother was admitted today with some chest pain and uncomfortable breathing. We've done some blood tests, a chest x-ray and monitored her heart, but everything seems to be fine."

"What was it then?"

"Does she suffer from anxiety at all? It's possible she had some sort of attack and couldn't stop it before it spiraled out of control."

"Yes, she definitely does. Well, when can I take her home?"

"We'll keep her overnight just to be certain, but you should be able to take her home tomorrow."

Relief swam through Emily, the worries that had plagued her the whole drive up now being put to rest.

"Thank you."

She collected her paperwork and headed back to her mum's house, another half an hour driving. She set herself up in the small guest bedroom and passed an uncomfortable night's sleep.

She messaged Nate to say goodnight, but he didn't respond.

THE NEXT DAY she took her mother home, cleaned her house, did some shopping for her and talked until she couldn't talk anymore. After they'd had dinner together, Emily got in her car and drove the four hours back home.

She was so relieved that her mother was all right, she could actually feel the tension in her muscles starting to slip away, giving her no anchor to hold onto.

When she arrived home around midnight, her exhaustion was such a complete thing that she crawled into bed and didn't surface for a full thirteen hours.

When she awoke, her head still ached and her belly burned with hunger. It was Saturday, but she couldn't possibly go into Eleanor's House today. She sent a quick message off to Cindy and promised to pop in tomorrow, once she'd rested. For herself, she needed to find out what was going on with Nate.

He hadn't responded to any of the three messages she'd sent him, and although she was dying to call him, she wasn't sure of the reception she would get.

Had running off to deal with her mother caused a flashback for him? Did he even have any family anymore?

Their relationship was still so new, and yet she could feel the potential for something great. If only he'd loosen the reins on whatever he was holding onto.

She blinked several times, accustoming them to the daylight streaming in through her curtains.

Breakfast and then Nate.

She made herself a smoothie and ate some fruit, the light meal exactly what she needed after two days of takeaway in a car.

When the clock struck ten she picked up her phone and rung Nate, her breath shuddering in her throat as she waited for him to pick up.

"Hey, Emily. How was your trip?"

His voice sounded stilted and a bit too professional considering the nights they'd shared, but she'd go along with it for the minute.

"Not too bad. Mum's heaps better, so I drove home late last night."

"You're back in Melbourne already?"

"Yep. I was hoping I could see you today and call in that raincheck from the other night. Do you want to come over and do dinner and a movie?"

The silence stretched for a moment. "I have dinner plans, unfortunately. Work related."

"Oh." The fact that he qualified dinner as work made her feel a little better, but she was still unsure on the sense of distance.

"You could come over later? I'll be home about ten."

"That would be great, Nate."

"See you then."

Emily hung up the phone with a sense of dread in her belly and a prickle of fear along her spine. Had he replaced whatever they'd started in the thirty-six hours she'd been unavailable?

She shook herself. She bloody hoped not.

It seemed silly to be so scared of losing what they'd just started to build. They hadn't been together long or shared enough. They hadn't even had the conversation of whether they were *together* or not. But Nathan Johnson was special, *too special* to step away from now.

11

———

She arrived at his apartment not long after ten, her belly full of pizza and her body feeling quite rested after another sleep.

She stepped up to the door and knocked. It opened within only a few seconds.

"Hey, Emmy." His voice sounded exhausted as he greeted her with a soft smile, wearing only jeans and a white singlet.

Her mouth went dry and she swallowed.

He was heart-wrenchingly beautiful when he looked this vulnerable. So *normal*, without his armor of sophistication.

She stepped in and closed the door, following him into the kitchen where the wine was already out. One glass and a fresh bottle of red, his glass of water nearby.

"Bad meeting?"

He ran a hand through his disheveled hair. "Ah, yeah. It wasn't exactly a work meeting. I know I said it was, but it was actually dinner with my uncle. Sorry."

She'd known a Saturday night dinner wouldn't be work, but didn't make a big deal out of the lie—obviously, he hadn't had a good night.

"Do you want a glass? You look like you could use a drink."

He shook his head hard. "No, thanks. But you go right ahead."

She smiled at him but didn't touch the alcohol. "Thanks. I'm fine."

Emily had a little look around the room as the conversation halted. All of his furniture and appliances were new and obviously expensive. The lack of personal touches was startling. His apartment was so very different than her own home.

Her eyes fixed on something strange in his pristine kitchen. She drifted over to it and lifted up the small cardboard box, her lips curving into a smile.

"You have to tell me. Why the obsession with the safety pins?"

Nathan shrugged, walking over and taking the box gently from her hands and sliding it back into its place as though it were a prized ornament that shouldn't be moved. Which was very strange. It had to be the cheapest thing in the whole apartment. "My mum used to give them to me."

Emily's breath caught in her throat. She didn't like the sound of that, but she needed to know the answer or her subconscious would torture her for days on what the reasons might be "Why? When?"

Again, that small shrug. "Anytime, really. But especially when she knew my father had gone out drinking."

The words *and would come back and beat the shit out of her* hung in the air. Emily cleared her throat and took a step closer to him.

"Bit of a dangerous thing to give to a child."

She tried for a light tone but her voice came out a little high and squeaky.

"Yes and no. I was eight and I learned to open them and pin them to my shorts or my top in rows. Great for fine motor control."

As though he wanted to demonstrate, he took two pins out of the box, one in each hand and opened them simultaneously.

"Wow, impressive."

He grinned and put them back.

Emily closed her eyes for a moment and then opened them again with a determination to work out what the answer actually was. She dove straight into the next part of the conversation, fully aware that she was pushing his boundaries and may pay for it.

"So… you carry them around because they make you feel safe?"

He frowned a little as he continued staring at the carpet. "It's better than most habits. Smoking, drinking."

She needed to take a deep breath but was scared of what that would do to the still, warm atmosphere in the room. He hadn't addressed the "safe" comment, but he didn't deny it either.

And why else would he keep one with him all the time?

"Since we're digging deep here, is there a story behind the fact you don't drink?"

Nate looked at her and opened his mouth, Emily assumed it was to refute the fact that he never drank alcohol. She raised one eyebrow and he shut his mouth again. "You know I have an eye for details, Nate."

He let out a huffy laugh. "Bloody solicitor…yeah, well. My father was an alcoholic. Enough said."

She knew there was more to the story than that and it was time to see what was behind door number two.

"Was that why he used to beat your mother, because he was always drunk?"

Nate's eyes zeroed in on hers. "Yeah, why?"

She shrugged and kept moving around the room, not always looking at him, but running her fingers along the edges of the furniture.

"I'm wondering why you restrict your world so much. You told me you never date women like me because you'd didn't think we're for real, that we're too much work, but what you mean is we need a lot of love, right?"

She kept her tone bright and looked back to see his quick nod as he crossed his arms over his chest and leaned back against the wooden desk.

"And loving someone is a problem for you, Nate?"

"I don't think so, but I've never really loved anyone before. Not in the romantic way you're talking about."

She didn't believe that. He didn't have the aura of someone who didn't care, who couldn't love. He had the feel of a person who'd loved, and lost. Lost big.

"You're kidding me? Never? Not even at high school or University? When you're young and fall so easily?"

He glanced away and she knew she'd hit a nerve. She didn't really want to know about the other women or woman who Nate had loved. But she knew it was essential to understanding him.

"Nate, you can tell me. Please, it's okay."

He took a deep breath, leaned back against one of the stone bench-tops and crossed his arms over his chest. "I did have a proper girl-friend once, and she liked to push all my buttons. No idea why. She could be so sweet, so kind, but then she'd get drunk and flirt with guys to make me jealous. The normal stupid things bitches do."

Emily swallowed hard as Nate's tone changed to one of callous-ness, but then, it was probably the best defense mechanism he had.

"Yeah, some women are pretty horrible. What happened to her?"

"We broke up."

"How come?"

"Because I almost hit her."

His tone, so cold and angry, hit her harder than his actual words.

"What?"

"What do you mean, what? I got drunk and she was being a horrible bitch. So I lifted my hand to hit her. We broke up then and there and I didn't really see her again."

Emily's head was spinning and all the strands of information weren't making total sense. Repeating things was the best way for her to understand what was going on. What was the core issue? He'd loved someone who made him feel like his father?

Oh shit, that would have been terrible. No wonder he'd practically sworn off women since.

"So, the one woman who you connected with, loved as much as one can love at age twenty-one, or whatever age you were, brought out a side of you that you didn't like, so you decided not to ever let anyone that close again?"

Nathan glared at her, not speaking, his nostrils flaring.

She probed a little deeper. "Does that sound right? Or am I misinterpreting what you're saying."

"You don't get it."

She kept her voice calm. She had to stay *calm*. "Then please explain it to me."

"She made me feel like my father, the man I hate most in this world. Why would I be with someone who brought that out in me?"

She'd been right. And what a terrible thing to face as a young man who'd lost his mother.

Yes, it all made sense, but his intimacy issues had to stem from somewhere. She'd always assumed it was because of his parents' abusive marriage.

"You wouldn't. No one would want to be with her. But you know you're not your father, don't you?"

"Of course, I do. I'm not my father, and it wasn't all her fault, either. I should never have been anywhere near that."

His voice had changed even more now. The syllables coming out like a growled mess.

She nodded and swallowed hard. She didn't know enough about the girlfriend to comment, but his defense of her meant that despite his words, he lay most of the blame on his own shoulders.

She didn't have much counselling experience and was now rethinking her wisdom on taking on this topic single-handedly.

"Of course, you're not. You're an incredible man, Nate. I admire you more than anyone in the world."

He rolled his eyes a little so she stepped closer to touch him. They'd gone past words now. She wanted to *show* him how much she trusted him, cared for him. "Don't you believe me?"

"I'm not that impressive, Emmy. I make decent money and I built Eleanor's House. No biggie compared to so many other self-made billionaires and philanthropists in this world."

She wound her arms around his waist and pressed her thighs against his. He didn't move into her contact, but he didn't push her away either. Encouraged, she pressed on.

"True, but I'm allowed to be a bit biased here. You didn't just build an incredible life from nothing. You survived a parent's death, an abusive environment, and thrived. There aren't too many self-made billionaires with your past, are there?"

A reluctant smile tugged up his lips.

"I suppose not, but still."

"Yeah, but still. I adore you and I know you are a good man, all the way down to your core."

She put both hands over his heart and pressed down to illustrate her point.

He grimaced and pulled away so that she had to step back and he could walk across the room.

"I might not be, Emmy. I might be capable of all the horrible things my father did. I'll never know unless I marry someone and let control go, drink maybe. I don't think I want to know."

"I don't think you are capable of being like your father. I know everyone is technically capable of anything in the wrong situation, the wrong environment. You got given lumps of coal for your life Nate, and you turned them into diamonds. I don't believe you would ever hurt me."

He shook his head at her, his eyes shining suspiciously. "I don't know why you trust me so much when I don't even trust myself."

"Maybe because I've seen all the good things you've done, and you focus on the bad? Maybe because I'm intuitive and trust my feelings. As I've said to you, only time is going to prove to you that I won't turn into a bitch, and I believe time is the only thing that will prove to you that you can love someone and still be the good person you work so hard on being."

Nathan ran a hand through his hair and let his head hang forward.

Emily's heart squeezed in her chest, robbing her of breath. She wanted to call out and bring back in the questions that were obviously tormenting him, but they needed to get to the bottom of this.

"My mother's death left a gaping hole in my heart, Emmy. I'm not sure you're right about me. I might not ever be what you need."

That was a change of conversation, but she'd go with it.

"One problem at a time. Has helping people filled the huge hole?"

"What do you mean?"

Emily swallowed hard and licked her dry lips. "It's a simple enough question, Nate. Do you feel fulfilled? Happy? Content? After all, you have single-handedly built Eleanor's House and maintained its staff and lodgings. You have given safety and support to more than ten thousand women and their children."

Nate's eyes widened. "That many already?"

"Didn't you listen at the anniversary?"

He shrugged, waving off her point with a flick of his hand.

"So what's your point, Emmy?"

She shivered at his use of her nickname. She loved how he called her something that no one else did, but pushed forward.

"Well, we need to fix that. If you want to help these women, you need to get involved more. That's how I fill the hole inside of me. I know it's nothing compared to what you and your mother went through, but I can't fix the injustice done to my parents, the guilt I feel at making heaps of money to pay off two houses. We need it, I know, however, it doesn't sit right. And each day I help another person at Eleanor's House, it makes me feel better."

"You seriously think the answer to my fears is getting more hand's on at Eleanor's House? After years of therapy, boxing and staying away from any woman who looked remotely nice, this is your solution?"

She laughed at his summary, stepping close to him again.

"Yes, and if it's not, we can try something else."

He grinned, grabbing her as she got closer and hauling her into his pelvis. "Taking you to bed will fix almost anything, I'm sure."

She twirled her arms around his neck and kissed him gently on the mouth. "Come with me to Eleanor's House tomorrow?"

He groaned and rolled his eyes. "Okay."

That was enough for her. She pressed into him harder, letting her tongue find his and her eyes close.

The time for speaking was done. She let him lead her to bed, where they undressed each other slowly, carefully. They kissed like their next breath might be their last, moaning and gasping as they shared their flavors and needs. She took her time exploring his body, licking his skin and savoring each groan she pulled from him.

Nate then turned his attentions on her, loving her body so thoroughly, tears leaked from her eyes as she climaxed.

She'd never felt so loved, appreciated, needed, than the moment he slid into her and gasped, his eyes on hers, and his body as close to hers as he could possibly be.

This time, she didn't even ask if she could stay. She just turned over, pulled his arms around her tightly and fell into a deep sleep.

Nate took a long, shuddering breath, and then another. He really didn't want to do this.

Stop being a pussy.

He nodded once to himself and tugged on his cufflinks at either wrist. He reached out his hand to the silver knob and pulled the door open. He'd designed that door, chosen that handle.

He moved inside and reached for the arrogance he knew was there to be had. The same confidence that had got him through a tough college degree, even harder job placements, and then building his own company from one room to a building full of people.

The new carpet looked good, and there was a surveyor looking at the walls for renovation. Great.

He stepped up and knocked on the door with the supervisor, Cindy Drummel's name in white letters across the wooden door.

"Hello, Cindy, I'm here to speak to some people about job prospects?"

The blonde woman turned towards him, squinting over her glasses as she stared up at him for a moment.

"Oh. Oh! Mr. Johnson, I'm so sorry I didn't greet you properly. We've been flat chat here today."

He smiled as the woman bustled around her desk that was overflowing with paperwork and shook his hand firmly. She reminded him of a mother hen, larger than life, warm and spoke far too much.

"Not a problem. Is Emily here?"

She should be. She left my warm bed on this freezing cold morning to volunteer.

"Yes, she arrived a few hours ago. Let's go see her."

He nodded and forced a smile to his lips as they moved into the heart of the center. His eyes focused on the architecture of the building. The skylight he'd had installed to keep the living areas bright. The architrave around the doors for a little bit of beauty and the heavy-duty carpets for the heavy foot traffic.

He'd thought about every single detail when he'd designed it over ten years ago and to see it all still looking so good made him feel quite proud.

"Nate!" Emily greeted him with a huge, sunny smile as she walked up to him.

His heart kicked out at him as love and familiarity washed over him in warm waves.

Damn. Not yet. Don't be in love with her already.

She didn't reach out and touch him, but his hands itched to grab her and kiss her. Last night had been amazing. Each kiss, each touch, every move from her eager body had made him want to come. The intensity was all-consuming.

"You came. I'm so glad."

"Yes, I decided you were right and I also spoke to Martine about it an hour ago." Which his executive assistant hadn't been too pleased with since it was a Sunday morning, but as always, she'd answered his call. "She recommended that we could hire some of the women who want some part-time work to help with reception, running errands, et cetera."

Which to him had sounded like a great idea. If he was serious about really helping the women at the shelter, then he may as well combine more of his business with the charity and vice versa.

"Oh, that's such a good idea. We can talk to some of them straight away. There's a group therapy session going on in one of the meeting rooms. Shall we go in there now?"

"That's fantastic, Mr. Johnson. Thank you." Cindy said next to him and Nate forced himself to nod and smile.

A sweat broke out on his forehead and he wiped it away, the heat in his cheeks making him rush over to a nearby table and pour himself a glass of water.

His hands were shaking and he reached for the safety pin in his pocket. His heart instantly calmed as he connected with the metal.

"You okay, Nate?" Emily asked as she stepped up next to him, her hand going to the crook of his elbow to offer some sort of support. He'd never known a woman who read him so well, and she seemed to actually care if he wasn't happy.

His heart was beating like a bongo drum in his chest. Boom. Boom. Boom.

He straightened his spine and gulped down the water before saying, "Yeah, of course. Right behind you."

She gave him one last worried look and headed off to the meeting room.

He had broached multi-million dollar deals when he'd been only twenty-eight years old, what on earth was he afraid of?

He shook himself and took another deep breath. Nothing to be afraid of. Absolutely nothing. These women weren't his mother and even if they were, what was wrong with that? She'd done her very best as his mother and had loved him. The best and only way she could.

The women in that room were the whole reason he'd raised all that money, donated so much time, and energy. Why wouldn't he want to see where the funds went?

Emily was waiting for him outside the room, her eyebrows furrowed into a frown.

"You know you don't have to do this if you really don't want to."

He shook himself hard. "No, you were right. This is why I set up Eleanor's House in the beginning. For these women."

And he had been avoiding the fruits of his labors as though they were poison apples. Why? When he'd succeeded with these women where he had failed with his mother.

She gazed up at him with that look she got sometimes which

meant she admired him, loved him maybe. Shiny, soft eyes and that gentle smile.

And all he could do was smile back because the thumping of his heart was so loud he could barely hear himself think.

They went through the door together and took a seat on the edge of the room, a small circle of women talking quietly in the center.

When he sat down, they all stopped speaking and practically cowered at his presence, shrinking into their chairs and curling their shoulders as they leaned towards each other for comfort.

Shit.

He hated this feeling. Like he was some big, violent male who might hurt them. He'd never do that. Never.

Maybe Emmy's right about me.

The woman, who he assumed was the counsellor, stood up and addressed him.

"I'm sorry, but this session is only for the women who seek refuge here. They aren't very comfortable with men around."

Yeah, and tall, alpha men like me are probably the worst sort.

He turned to Emily with a resigned sigh and she gave him a hesitant smile back. He'd just realized another reason he chose strong, bitchy, confident women. They never made him feel powerful or strong, big or clumsy. He didn't need to control himself with them because they didn't see him for who he actually was.

Here. With broken, big-hearted women, he felt who he was. What he was.

"Let's go, Emmy."

She stood up and addressed the group.

"I'm not sure if any of you were here for our ten-year anniversary last week, but this is Nathan Johnson, owner and founder of Eleanor's House."

The women's eyes grew as big as planets and their mouths gaped open.

He slid back in his chair and let his shoulders relax. Okay, so maybe he'd assumed wrongly. Or maybe Emily saw him for more than what he looked like on the outside?

Emily continued speaking, gesturing to him. "I know this isn't strictly protocol, Jeanie, but Nathan simply wanted to come and see what good was being done at the center that he has single-handedly supported for all of us."

Wow. Okay.

The woman flushed a rose pink and indicated to the circle. "Well, then please join us. I, myself, need to thank you for the opportunity this center afforded me, Mr. Johnson."

Emily grabbed his hand and dragged him onto a chair in the inner circle so that he faced the six women, all of them now with relaxed body language and soft smiles on their faces.

Holy shit.

He stared at them for a moment, unable to process the difference in the women now that they knew what he was, or who he was.

"You don't need to do that."

The counsellor continued. "Oh, but I do. All the women know my story. I was abused for years by my husband and was running away from him through the city one night when I literally fell over the mat on the front doorstep of Eleanor's House. This center saved me, and now I get to use my skills as a healer to help other people get through their darkest hours."

Nathan wiped at his brow and shrugged out of his jacket. There was no air in this room, he needed to install better ventilation.

He nodded his thanks to the counsellor and she gestured to the women in the group.

"Who would like to share next?"

A small red-headed woman with a nasty bruise on one side of her face timidly held up her hand.

"Yes, Macey, please share whatever you would like to tell us."

"I'm ready to talk about this night." She gestured to her face and everyone nodded.

Nathan swallowed hard, tugging at his cufflinks again as his shirt stuck to his sweaty skin. He glanced around at the women with cardigans and warm jumpers. What was wrong with them? Wasn't everyone in the room boiling?

"I came home from doing a double shift and he was drunk, as usual. He was always drunk. I walked into the kitchen to get something to eat and he began banging on the kitchen cupboards to scare me and make me jump." She glanced around the circle while wrapping her slim arms around herself. "He liked doing that. I don't know why. But anyway, I ignored him and tried to open the fridge, but he wanted a password. I didn't know it but guessed a few times to humor him. On the third guess, he hit me."

Nate began to tremble—the woman's fear that night a palpable thing to him. His mother would scoop him up, no matter where he was, and lock him in his bedroom when she heard his father pull into the driveway. Certain nights he'd drink with his mates from work and somehow Nate's mum would always know.

The banging front door would signal he was home and Nate would hide under his bed, or in the cupboard. As he got older he found some earphones to play music with, but it never completely blocked out the noise of her screams and his father's violence.

So scared. So helpless.

Nausea rolled in his stomach as the young woman relived the blows, the fear, the panic. The monumental moment when he finally stopped so she could crawl away to safety.

He'd often wondered what his mother had actually gone through on those nights. He'd seen the bruises and blood the next day and had to ignore what it really meant. She'd never talked about it and he'd never really thought about it.

But sitting here with these women meant he couldn't ignore it any longer.

His mother had been weak, terrified and alone.

I'm going to be sick.

Nate jumped up and rushed to the corner of the room, hot stomach acid rushing out of him as he shivered and fought the need to curl up into a ball.

He wiped at his mouth and stuck his hand in his pocket, reaching for the safety pin that was always there for him.

As he turned and got to his feet he saw that the women were all standing also, a mixture of horror and pity on their sad faces. Emily rushed forward but he held up his hands, sweat dripping down the side of his face.

"No."

He'd reached his limit today. He couldn't handle any more. Certainly not from *her*.

He forced his legs to move and he made it to his chair, just. He nodded once at the counsellor and grabbed his jacket. He held tight to his dignity and staggered out of Eleanor's House.

When his feet found the sidewalk he took off running and didn't stop until he'd reached his apartment block, where he climbed, suit and all, into his large bed. He didn't get out for almost a day.

12

———

"Thanks, Martine. If he comes in today, could you let him know I've called again?"

"Yeah, sure, sweetie. See you on Friday?"

"Yes, of course. See you then."

It had been two days since Nate's meltdown at Eleanor's House and Emily couldn't even find him. He wasn't answering emails, phone calls or even house calls. He hadn't turned up to work if Martine was to be believed, and Emily was literally worried sick.

She'd pushed him, and look what had happened.

She didn't know whether to laugh or cry, but she hadn't eaten properly in days and her stomach still didn't feel right.

An email pinged in her inbox and she opened it, holding her breath as Johnson Property Development came up on her screen.

Emily, Nathan has come into work today but he has told me to block all of your calls and to find a way out of your contract so that we can hire someone else to work here.

I obviously have not got permission to reveal this, but I know him well, and he is not his normal self at all. What happened?

Emily didn't even think twice, she just set her fingers to the keys and tried to explain to the woman who was closest to Nathan what had happened.

Thank you so much for emailing me, Martine. I understand what you're saying and I won't tell him.

I have been worried sick that he may have been ill or worse.

We had a chat the other night and I suggested that he might be happier with his life if he saw the wonderful things he did with his money and Eleanor's House. So he came to the center on the weekend and sat in on a counselling group.

He only stayed for about ten minutes, vomited and left. I think he had some sort of panic attack.

She stopped, re-read the email and then sent it on.

A moment later another popped up.

Oh crap, you have no idea what you've done. He's never dealt with his mother's abuse, or her death, and if this has popped the lid on that, then he needs some serious help.

Will keep you in the loop.

Martine.

Now she was the one that was going to be sick.

Emily rushed to the bathroom and stuck her head over a toilet, her belly rolling in pain as she heaved up her breakfast, tears leaking from her eyes.

Oh, yuck.

She spat into the toilet and flushed, walking out to wash her hands and her face and examine the mess in the mirror.

What had she done?

Would he ever forgive her for trying to help? Her intentions had been right, but would that be enough to get him to forgive her?

She stared into the mirror and a wave of nausea rolled over her again.

I don't think it's going to be enough.

EMILY LET NATE have his silence for two very long days. She owed him space and time, but what he didn't realize was, she was giving him her sanity as well.

She'd worked until midnight both nights so she didn't have to go home and deal with the silence her big, empty house afforded. Once her refuge, now it mocked her. She'd wanted money and a home that she could support herself. She'd got exactly what she wanted, stability and comfort, and how cold it was without the man she wanted in her bed beside her.

On Friday she dressed carefully, wearing the suit he'd bought her, doing her hair and makeup with much more care than she usually would.

She'd barely stepped in the door and opened her computer when she saw three emails from Martine waiting for her in her inbox.

Dear Ms. Sanders,

Please find enclosed your letter of contract cancellation.

I am sorry to inform you that we no longer require your services but wish you all the best in the future.

Kind Regards

The team at Johnson Property Development.

Hot tears tingled at the back of her nose and she sniffed rapidly to dispel them. She wasn't letting him do this.

The second email was a bit different.

Em,

You need to fix this. He's acting like a bear with a sore paw and I know I'm not the cure!

But the third one made her cry out with glee and snatch up her bag.

Okay, I've scheduled a false meeting at ten so he doesn't leave the office. Get your ass over here now!

She glanced at the clock on her laptop. It was 9:10 a.m.

She made her excuses to her boss and ran out the door. It was only a short walk to Nate's office and she needed the time to clear her head.

She slowed her pace and took long breaths of cool, winter air. She wasn't sure what she'd done to get Martine on her side, but she would, quite literally, be eternally grateful for her help.

She arrived with plenty of time to spare so went to the bathroom to freshen herself up and get a strong handle on her emotions.

Nate was going to toss her out on her ass, and she had to be ready for that. He was terrified of getting too close to anyone, that was damn obvious, but the *why* wasn't so much. If she could get him to open up, let her in some more, she could love him how he deserved to be loved.

Whoa, when did that happen?

She closed her eyes for a moment and let the truth sink in. She'd fallen head over heels for the complex, brilliant man that Nate was.

The only important thing now was to apologize, and grovel if necessary, for him to forgive her.

A groan escaped her lips and she mumbled to herself, "Yeah, but you've gotta make him talk to you first."

She moved with a brisk stride and purpose, out the door, along the corridor and through the maze of floors until she stood outside Nate's door.

Her belly trembled, her hands were sweating and the need to run was there in the shaking of her legs.

She lifted her hand and knocked on the door before she could change her mind.

"Come in."

Her tummy dropped at the sound of his strong, autocratic tones but she pushed open the door. She'd conquered bigger feats than this. She could apologize to the man who meant way more to her than she'd like to admit.

"Good morning, Nate."

He froze in his chair, his eyes like ice as they looked her up and down.

She lifted her chin and gave him her sunniest smile as she strode straight in and sat in the chair facing him.

His eyes were hard and angry as he stared at her. Dr. Jekyll was back.

"Emily. Are you here to sign your termination papers?"

May as well agree to that.

"Yes. I'm also here to talk to you about Sunday morning and to talk about us."

"Us?" His tone would have caused icicles to grow in Hell. She actually shivered as cold tingles quivered over her spine.

"Yes. Us. We had an amazing night together Saturday night and then Sunday morning was terrible. I hope that's not going to ruin everything between us."

He stood up and she got to her feet also. There was no way she could stay sitting while he glowered down at her.

"First of all, Emily, there is no us. We slept together a few times and now it's over."

Cra-ack goes my heart.

She waited, not breathing. Was that all he was going to say? He couldn't possibly be that upset still? She'd been really hoping he would forgive her for Sunday.

"That's a bit harsh, Nate. I know I shouldn't have pushed you into that room on Sunday morning, it was a mistake. I won't do that again. But please, let me make it up to you."

He walked around the desk and strode over to the opaque window and stood next to the door. She half expected him to open it and demand she leave, but he was obviously getting into position.

She twisted to face him, her heart thumping in her chest. She tried hard not to show him that she was in pain, but her face always belied her feelings and she knew he'd be able to see more than she wanted him to.

"Emily, I am not some project that you need to work on. I am not a charity case. Please get out of my office and take your meddling ways with you."

He still didn't open the door and her mouth dropped open.

"Pardon me? I never thought you were a charity case. Far from it. You're one of the most successful, humble, beautiful people I've ever met. You're perfect the way you are."

A muscle ticked in his jaw and he glanced away.

"Get out."

No, please don't, Nate.

She stepped closer, tears gathering in her eyes as her nose began to sting. She swallowed down the lump that had risen in her throat and tried to blink back the warmth in her eyes.

"Nate, I'm sorry. I didn't mean to make you feel that way. I should never have pushed you to face your fears like that, it wasn't fair. I just thought… I didn't intend to…" She was losing the battle, she could feel it in the crispness of the air, in the straightness of his spine.

"No, you didn't intend to do anything. You didn't try to empathize with me, despite everything I explained, Emily. I let you in closer than I've ever let anyone, and yet it still wasn't enough. You treated me like one of your Eleanor's House women, and I am not yours to fix!" He puffed a little and glared at her hard.

Her throat hurt, her heart ached, and she couldn't speak.

He took a deep breath and seemed to gather his composure before speaking again. "I'm giving you a week's notice to finish up at Eleanor's House too, and I suggest you don't push me any further or I will speak to your supervisor at your day job as well."

His nostrils were flaring and goosebumps rose on her skin. Dr. Jekyll really was out today, and he had a knife aimed right at her heart. She stepped away a little, finding her voice once again.

"But Eleanor's House is my life. It's the best thing I do with my time. I love it."

And I love you. I'm so sorry I did this to us, Nate.

"Find another charity."

He opened the door and lifted his chin even higher.

She had nothing left to say. All the words had been said.

She reached for a smile but found nothing left inside herself. She could volunteer at another charity, of course. She'd have to. She needed to offset the guilt she felt for the money she made in her corporate job, and helping really good-hearted people made her feel good about herself.

People who needed her.

Which, it was quite obvious, Nate didn't.

"Thank you, Mr. Johnson. And good luck with everything."

Her voice sounded a lot stronger than she felt and she was proud of herself for not collapsing completely as he nodded once in dismissal. She pushed her legs to walk her body to the lift and to push the button.

The yellow light lit up and her world swayed on its axis.

One day was all it had taken to turn her life upside down, one morning, one single minute in time. And as she stood by the lift waiting for her carriage to arrive the first of many, many tears slipped down her cheeks.

She'd just ruined the best thing in her life, and for the first time, she had no idea how to fix it.

13

———

*E*ating alone used to fill him with a sense of power. Happiness. Relaxation.

Very strange that it now made him feel like a loser, even in an expensive restaurant.

How could one woman make such a difference in his life?

Nathan finished his dinner and wandered along King Street, the lights and music of a strip joint calling to him like the virtual siren call it was trying to be.

Why not?

He stepped into the well-lit, clean establishment and made his way to the bar. He ordered a drink from the young girl behind the bar and turned to enjoy the show. There were girls giving lap dances in corners, groups of men surrounding the stage, and several solo older men that made him frown.

He'd never enjoyed strip joints, even in University when his friends had dragged him out for a night on the town. After a lifetime of watching his mother get degraded, the last thing he wanted to do was watch other women sell their bodies for money.

Then why had he come in?

He paid for his whiskey and took a seat on the barstool. Something had drawn him inside. Pity and depression, perhaps?

For fuck's sake, pull yourself together. It's only been a week.

The whiskey was strong and burned his throat as he swallowed it down.

One drink and he'd leave.

A hand slid across his thigh and he turned to give the girl the brush off but froze as boiling hot lava slid down his spine.

"Sharnie?"

The weathered face before him registered who he was with a gaping mouth and a loud gasp.

"Nathan? Natey…? Is it really you?"

He grimaced at the old nickname that she'd used on him back in Uni. He'd hated it then and now it was ridiculous.

"Sharnie, how are you? Long time no see."

She slid up closer to him, her undernourished body wrapped in ill-fitting underwear, not a sight he wanted to see. She'd always been thin, but now her skin was sagging, her body wearing out faster than it should have been at thirty-six.

"Oh fabulous, darling, just fab. I always wondered what happened to you after we broke up."

Nathan straightened up on his barstool. Nothing good had happened after they broke up. He'd spent years torturing himself over who he'd become with Sharnie and at one stage he'd tried to find her, but she'd disappeared off most people's radars. Now he knew why.

"Have you got time to talk?"

Sharnie looked around. There were more than enough girls for the men in the room. She turned back to him with a smile that didn't reach her eyes.

"Sure, I'm due a cigarette break. Wanna come stand outside with me for a ciggy?"

He tried not to show his revulsion as he nodded and they made their way outside. He hated cigarette smoke more than most things. His father had smoked.

"So, what has my old lover done with his life?"

She lit her cigarette, licked her lips and looked up at him with shrewd, blue eyes. He stared at her for a moment, comparing her to the memory he held so tightly to his chest. She was very different now. The sweet, beautiful girl he'd known was gone.

"I'm an architect." *And a billionaire, but you probably shouldn't know that.*

Which she should remember since he'd been doing his course when they were dating. "I own my own business."

"Woo-hoo, you have done well for yourself, haven't you?" She ran a hand down his arm in a lecherous way.

"Yeah, I've done all right for an orphan."

Which was technically untrue—his dad was alive, somewhere. But as far as he was concerned, he had no family.

"What happened to us, Natey? I was so convinced we were going to stay together forever. You broke my heart when you ended it all."

Her tone was smooth as she sidled up next to him, those once warm blue eyes, cold as frosted glass.

He tried to step away but she pressed even closer. Had the years of stripping and living on the edge done this to her? Or had she always been so cold? He couldn't remember now. The memories were starting to blur.

"We broke up because I almost hit you, remember? During that fight? I was terrified I'd do it again. That you were too sweet to deal with me."

Or that his love and passion for her had turned him into his father.

She cackled out a laugh, then coughed harshly.

When she'd drawn breath, she took another drag on the cigarette, dropped it to the ground and pressed it into the bitumen with her red shoe.

"Sweet? Me? I was always the one to start the fights. Don't you remember? I loved it when you got all angry and jealous. It showed me how much you cared about me."

She pouted and got closer, fluttering her fake eyelashes at him.

What the...

"Pardon? Weren't you devastated when we had that fight?"

She laughed again. "Hardly. I thought you'd stay with me for sure after that, but you never came back."

He staggered away and pressed his spine against the bluestone building wall as his knees began to give out. No, that couldn't be true. Why would a woman want that sort of connection with him? Could he have chosen any worse?

"What's the problem, sugar? Are you still into that? Cause I can handle a beating now, I can tell you. My last few guys always hit me when I bitched at them too much. Turns into really hot sex, too."

She advanced on him like a panther, pushing aside her black coat to reveal the swing of her hips. "I remember how you like it. I'm sure I can still turn you on."

He put a hand up to ward her off. His head spinning like a top, round and around. "What are you talking about? I always thought you were some sweet innocent that I'd hurt. I didn't forgive myself."

She ran a hand down to his crotch, squeezing gently. "I can be anything you want, Natey. Your sweet, little, innocent girl again. No problem."

He looked straight at her, needing the truth so much. If he'd been wrong all these years, then he needed to know.

"But the alcohol, me almost hitting you. I thought I was like my father. That I couldn't cope with being in love."

She shrugged her shoulders. "Listen, Natey. I have to go make some money. Are you gonna come pay for a lap dance, or what?"

She turned her nose up at him, as he straightened to his full height and pulled out his wallet. He checked the contents and pulled out two green bills.

"I'll give you two hundred dollars if you can give me an honest answer."

She practically salivated over the notes he had in his hands, her beady gaze going from his fingers to his eyes and back again.

"I'll tell you anything you want, Natey."

"Stop calling me that. It's Nathan!"

She nodded, not taking her eyes off the money.

He growled and thrust the cash into her hands. "Now answer truthfully. You've already got the money, so I'm not paying for a specific answer, I just need to know. Was it me? Was I the evil one who almost hit a sweet, innocent young girl that night? Do I poison everyone I love?"

She cocked her head at him and sniffed. "I don't know what you're on, man. You were hot and going to be rich. I kicked myself for years for not landing you properly like I should have." She shrugged. "The night you mean, I pushed you as hard as I could. I wanted a hard fucking, or break up-makeup sex. Something. Anything. I just wanted to see some real passion in you, and instead, you bloody left. If you thought I was some sweet little blonde, it was your own fault."

She slipped her money into a small purse she held and winked at him. "You sure you don't want anything else?"

From you? Never. He shook his head and waved her off.

When she finally left, he pushed himself off the wall and began walking. His head was spinning like he'd consumed a whole bottle of whiskey, but he had to keep moving or he'd collapse.

All those years...

All those years he'd thought he was a true bastard on the inside. That he could become his father with a drink in his hand. It was all wrong.

So many lost moments, so many chances he hadn't taken.

Emily.

He tripped and caught himself on a light pole, his heart pounding his sternum like a hammer on an anvil.

He was going to be sick again.

His stomach burned as he retched into a nearby bin.

Gross. It was becoming a bad habit.

He wiped his mouth and kept running. He needed to get home. Everything he thought about himself had been wrong.

Emily had been right. He wasn't a bad person.

I love her.

Nathan started running, his legs aching as he pumped the strong muscles as hard as he could.

Thank you, God.

Whatever had pushed him into that strip joint tonight had saved his life, and his future.

He panted hard as he turned a corner and kept running. He needed to escape his demons and his past. Hoping to leave it all behind on the dirty streets of King Street where it belonged.

NATHAN HAD to make it up to Emily, but how? Just turn up at her home and apologize? No. It had to be bigger than that. The official grand gesture.

Not that he'd done anything in a past relationship that resembled *anything* close to a grand gesture, but he understood the merit behind it.

He made a few calls and found out it was Emily's last shift at Eleanor's House on Sunday. Despite his one week's notice, she seemed to have stretched the time to ten days.

Good.

He'd spent his adult life mourning his mother's death and damning himself for being like his father. He'd been wrong and stupid.

He was done wallowing in self-pity.

It ended. Now.

He spent all week getting on top of his work and setting up a few days off for the following week. Assuming Emily forgave him, he was taking her away for a few days to get acquainted once again with that beautiful body of hers.

A ripple of lust shimmied through his belly at that idea. It had been too long since he'd felt the clasp of her hot body around him, those beautiful eyes staring up at him.

He waited until six o'clock at night, having been in contact with Cindy for much of the day. He'd never really considered the good women in this world, having ignored them for most of his adult life. But Cindy was a good woman, as was Emily, and he was supremely grateful to have them in his life.

As he stepped back over the threshold of his charity house, a sense of peace settled over him. He hadn't been able to save his mother from his father's abuse, he'd been just a kid at the time.

It was time to forgive himself and take a proper look at what he'd done with his life. His money and hard work had helped a lot of other women's lives, and he was damn proud of it.

He moved through the house, smiling at the women who gaped at him from the sidelines. He'd deliberately worn a polo shirt and some jeans, hoping that by dressing down he'd appear less intimidating.

It wasn't really working, but he wasn't giving up. They may need to put some photos up around the place so the women got used to his appearance and didn't mind him popping in.

Stepping up to the door, he remembered the panic attack he'd had two weeks ago, and he smiled at the difference in him today. He had to admit, just standing on the stoop made his heart pound a little faster than normal, but he pushed through the uncomfortable feeling and opened the door. He moved through the charity and opened another door, interrupting a meeting he knew Emily would be at. In fact, it was a small party they'd organized to say goodbye to her. There was a table with cakes and drinks being served. Very similar to the anniversary night.

"Nathan! So glad you made it." Cindy rushed across the room in a flurry of perfume and he let her take his arm and pull him to the front of the room.

Emily was staring at him with a wounded expression in her eyes.

"Ah. Mr. Johnson, I know it's slightly longer than a week, but I had to tie up some loose ends with open cases and I—"

He cut her off as quickly as possible. "I came here tonight to let everyone know that there's no need for this party. If Emily wishes to continue to volunteer at Eleanor's House forever, we would be honored to have her."

A cheer went up and he let his eyes focus on her. The beautiful woman in front of him who had never given up on him.

Her mouth had fallen slightly open and she seemed frozen, despite everyone around her jumping up and down and trying to hug her.

She stepped forward, a frown pulling down her soft pink lips. "I don't understand."

"Emily, I was wrong." Three words he'd never said aloud. It was amazing how easy they were to say. "You belong here, and I'm sorry I tried to force you out because of my own shit."

There was a titter and a few gasps that flowed through the group of women. He put his hand out to her.

She took it and he pulled her to the side of the group, knowing full well that everyone could hear, and not giving a damn if they did.

"Forgive me for being a jackass about everything. You know I come with a few too many scars, but I'm working on them."

She reached for his chest, clinging to the cotton as tears gathered in her eyes.

"What? No, I'm the one that should be sorry! I was so insensitive to how you felt. I can't believe I did all those things to you. After everything you've suffered, I just went and made it worse for you, when all I wanted to do was love you."

Her voice broke and he pulled her tighter into his arms.

"Shall we go home and talk about it? Or do you have more things to tidy up here?"

"She can go," Cindy said from behind Emily, winking at him with a knowing smile.

"Great. Thanks, ladies. I'll see you through the week perhaps?"

He'd spoken to Cindy about getting some counselling done himself. After his mother's death and his father's alcoholism, he was in need of a bit of help, and he was finally man enough to admit it.

"Back to your apartment, Nate?" Emily's voice was small as they walked outside into the fresh air.

He pressed his lips to hers, unable to stand to look at her without kissing her a moment longer. A shiver ran through her and he pulled away. They both needed to be as close as possible, he knew that. Skin to skin, heart to heart. And they weren't going to get that out on the street.

"It's closest."

She nodded and he pulled her away to his car which he'd parked on the street. In mere moments, he'd have Emily in his home and back to his bed, where she belonged.

14

———

*S*he'd said she loved him—sort of.

Oh, crap.

Emily stepped into Nathan's apartment feeling better than she had in two weeks. She'd been feeling so sad, so cut off from the world. All the sunshine had gone out of her life, and now that it was back, she was almost giddy with the relief. He'd forgiven her for all the stupid mistakes she'd made.

His voice was smooth and sexy as it slid into her ear. "Let's get to bed so I can show you how much I've missed you."

Oh yes, please.

He pulled her into his bedroom and began shucking off his clothes.

She wanted him so badly, and as his polo shirt disappeared and then his belt, her mouth literally watered. He was so beautiful, inside and out, but she still had so many unanswered questions.

"Does that mean you want to go back to how we were?"

He shook his head and her stomach plummeted. What did that mean?

"I want a lot more than that. I want you here all the time. I want to start a real relationship, where I have you in my life and in my bed every night."

No way.

He reached for her coat and tugged it off, removing her blouse and bra before she'd even gotten her brain to make sense of his last statement.

"But, how did this happen?"

Nate kicked off his shoes and threw his jeans across the room.

He stood before her naked. Beautifully, deliciously, gorgeously, *naked.*

"I realized I was living in the past, and fighting ghosts and shit that just don't exist anymore."

He reached for her and she slid her hands up his arms, feeling the heat of his body beneath her palms. Had he really been fighting his demons while she'd been in her own depressive black cloud?

"So you're ready for a better future?"

He kissed her lips briefly, tasting of desire and heated male.

"Yes. With you. Absolutely."

He pushed her onto the bed and began pulling down her pants, kissing her belly, her thighs, her knees, as he went.

Then went her knickers, flying across the room to join the rest of their clothes.

Wow, he's in a rush tonight.

He crawled up the bed and slid between her thighs, his hot, naked skin against hers. His huge body on top of hers, weighing her down and grounding her on this earth.

I am so lucky to have him.

She stared up into his eyes and sensed something new, deep within herself. An awareness of a huge flush of heat radiating from him, as though a part of his soul wanted to blend with hers.

He ran his half-hard cock up and down her split, spreading the moisture and licking his fingers to add more. Heat and blood swirled around her belly, readying itself for him.

Was he going to make love to her already?

"I want to be inside you."

She nodded, opening her legs further for him. She heard the words he didn't say. There would be no fancy foreplay, no positions that meant they could hide their faces from one another.

It was just the two of them, sharing their love for each other.

He slid inside her and lay on top so that her breasts pressed against his chest and her pelvis cradled his hips. He began rocking his hips slowly as he stared down at her.

She hadn't thought it would be possible to make love like this, but as her belly started to tighten and his kisses got deeper, she began to believe in the impossible.

She needed to get closer to him. She lifted her body up and wrapped herself around him in every way she could, her legs around his hips, her arms around his back and she squeezed his cock with pulses of her internal muscles.

"Oh wow, Emily. That feels incredible."

He began moving a little faster, kissing her nose, her lips, her cheeks. Sweat slicked his back as the air around them became more heated, filled with their moans and the sounds of their bodies moving together.

He was getting harder and longer inside her. But there was something else there as well. With each thrust, each roll of his hips, she felt the swell of love hitting her. Like a wave against the shore, but she could accept it and push it back.

She lifted her lips and kissed him deeper, squeezing him tighter as she tasted his tongue, and began to come. It hit her like a truck, no warning, just *bam*.

She cried out as her body locked down on him. Pleasure coursed through her body like a hot river, passing over her from head to toe. She rode the crest up and over until she opened her eyes and looked up at him again.

Amazing.

His eyes had darkened, his mouth set.

"Damn, I wanted to come with you so badly then."

He moved faster, setting his lips to her neck and speaking into her ear.

"I love you, Emily." She gasped and grabbed him tighter.

"I love you too, Nate. So much." Tears welled and flowed, her throat tightening as hot emotions blanketed her body. She dug her nails into his back. Wanting him even deeper.

"I love who you are, I love how you see me, I love that I want to be a better person around you."

He was saying all the words she'd dreamed of and never thought she'd hear. She clung tight to him, terrified to let go lest he disappear into the night like the fantasy he was now becoming.

Her body tightened once more as the swell of love rose and fell. He began to slam into her she came again, an orgasm rolling through her as her heart squeezed tight.

"Ah... oh God, Nate."

He groaned, deep in his throat and moved even faster, that swell of love rolling into her again and again.

"One day. When we are ready. I'm going to make you pregnant."

She gasped and held tighter to him, her belly clenching tightly as his words wove a spell around her.

She already wanted that so badly. How could he want it too?

"I will squirt inside you, everything I am. And I will give you a baby."

She screamed out this time as her rolling orgasms continued, smacking into her so hard she arched her back and dug her nails into his shoulders.

His moan rang in her ears but he kept thrusting into her.

"You want that, Emmy. Don't you? Tell me you want my baby, our baby."

She couldn't lie about that. With her love for him came the need for a family, a future, a baby with his eyes.

"Yes, Nate. Yes, yes, yes."

He lifted his head and captured her mouth with his, kissing her and groaning in his throat as his orgasm hit.

He held tight to her hips and as he pulsed inside her, her body clamped down on him, milking up his seed.

She screamed out again, her whole body shuddering with the most intense orgasm of her life. He relaxed onto her, both of them still moaning and twitching. A messy heap of sweat and gasps, tangled limbs and red faces.

"Thank you." His words whispered across her cheek as he settled on top of her, shifting his weight a little so that he was still inside of her, but she could relax.

"No, my beautiful man. Thank you. For everything."

She nestled into him and closed her eyes, feeling completely safe and loved in the circle of his arms. Her man, her hero, her love.

EPILOGUE

12 months later.

"Look Eleanor, sweetie. Daddy's cutting the ribbon on his new House."

Emily lifted up her barely awake three-month-old daughter, the baby they'd conceived the night he'd declared his love for her. They both watched with pride as her husband cut the red ribbon tied to the front door of the second Eleanor's House in Australia. This one in Sydney.

A roar of applause went up around them as Nathan shook the mayor's hand and opened the door to his exquisite new building. Three months in the planning and five months of renovations, but they were here, and she couldn't be prouder.

"Let's go see Daddy."

She held her daughter tighter to her chest as she stepped up the three marble steps and gave her brilliant husband a huge smile.

"Congratulations, Nate. I am so proud of you."

He glanced away with a huge smile on his face.

"Stop it, Emmy. You know you've put in just as much work as me on this project."

"That is so not true." Once she'd gotten to seven months pregnant, she'd had to stop so many of her work duties. And after giving birth to Eleanor three months ago, she'd stopped all the flights, phone calls and site visits Nate had very much done this all on his own.

"I would never have done this without you."

He gestured widely to the people milling around, all exclaiming at the building and its features.

She smiled up at him, her big, strong hero. "We make a great team."

He nodded at her. "That we do."

He bent his head to kiss her and then to Eleanor's rosy little cheeks.

Nate was an attentive and loving father, although his original reservations about fatherhood had been understandable. Working with Cindy closely had helped him overcome most of his obstacles.

"Would you like a tour, my lady?"

"I would, kind sir."

She bobbed a curtsy and he laughed, a lovely rich sound that she missed when he was away.

They walked inside and she got lost in the whirlwind of information and enthusiasm from Nate. He now loved his charity work just as much as his property development. He was happy, he was strong, and as the woman by his side, she couldn't be prouder of being the one who healed the heart of her hero.

THE END

Thank you so much for reading 'Good Girl.'
I hope you enjoyed it as much as I enjoyed writing it!
If you enjoyed these characters, I think you will love my latest release:

If you would like to hear more about my coming releases,
Please sign up to my newsletter here!
https://www.subscribepage.com/f9e0a1

www.ingramcontent.com/pod-product-compliance
Lightning Source LLC
Chambersburg PA
CBHW062310200726
48292CB00004BA/1498